The Lord Mammon

Kyuka Lilymjok

ISBN: 978-978-069-689-4

Published by:
Free Pen Publishers
10 Lachlan Close Maitama, Abuja

To my wife Maria and my children: Justice, Sunfair and Fairprincess

The son of a witch shall sit
On the throne of the heart
The mind shall be his servant
Worry not Satan that you are old
Sick or dead, or that you never existed
Your grandson is out there bending men to your
will

Chapter One

And I behold another beast coming out of
the earth
And he has two horns like a lamb
And he spoke like a dragon
And he doeth great wonders
So that he maketh fire come down from
heaven
On earth in the sight of men

And deceived them that dwelt on earth
By means of those miracles which he had
power to do
In the sight of the beast
Saying to those that dwelt on earth that they
should
Make an image to the beast
Which had the wound on the head and did
live

And he had power to give life
Unto the image of the beast
That the image of the beast
Should both speak and cause that as many as
Would not worship the image of the beast
Should be killed

And he causeth all:

Both small and great, rich and poor, free and bound

To receive a mark on the right hand or on their foreheads

And that no man might buy or sell
Save him that had the mark or the name of the beast
For it is the number of a man
And his number is six hundred and sixty-six.

'This is the frightening prophecy of the Bible for the end times,' Pastor Gojang reeled on the pulpit, stabbing the air with his Bible held firmly in his right hand.

Many hearts in the congregation shuddered at the afflictions of the last days the Bible prophesied about. Only a few hearts retained their Sunday peace and put up bright faces that seemed to say, 'we are not partakers of the evil days to come. We are believers of Christ who cannot be harmed by the old enemy. When this Armageddon does come, we will be in a new world of God which saved Noah of old from the apocalypse of his day.'

'In conference with his disciples, Jesus told them the secrets of the kingdom of heaven have been revealed to only a few chosen ones,' Pastor Gojang continued after a long pause he appeared to be in communication with heaven. 'What I am about telling you is one of the secrets of heaven that has been revealed to me. The beast in the verses we just read is a literal and metaphorical beast. The literal beast is a monster that would come at the end of time. The metaphorical beast is money, which is already here with us. The beast God revealed to John in the verses we read comes from the earth and money is on earth. The beast does a lot of wonders and money does a lot of wonders. The beast deceives those who dwell on earth; so, does money. Men worship the beast; so do they money. Small and great, rich and poor, free and bound all receive the mark of the beast on the right hand or on their foreheads; so do all these classes of people carry money with them. No one can buy or sell in the market save he that has the mark or name of the beast. No one can buy or sell in a market that has no money. I can go on and on,' he pontificated and paused for what he said to sink into the minds of his flock.

'In the verses we read, money is the beast while the love of it the mark of the beast,' he went on with the fervent mien of a man who had recently held discussions with God. 'The beast does not take a man to hell. In fact, the beast can be used to help the needy and spread the gospel. When used for these good purposes, money is no longer the beast but *holy water*. It is the love of money – the mark of the beast that is a passport to hell. The love of money turns the hand of a man into a fist that sprinkles no *holy water*. A fist, let it be known, is a barren ground. Nothing comes out of it. It is a pregnancy that delivers no succor for anyone; it is a bulge of heartlessness; it is a bud that does not burst open for bees to gather honey; it is a forehead with the mark of the beast. No man can worship God or bless another with a fist. As it is with man, it is with God. God does not bless people with fists but with open palms. It is the open palms a man worships God with or uses to bless other people that God uses to bless him. A man with the mark of the beast either on his forehead or hand is a worshiper of Mammon. For him, it is *to hell o Israel*. No doubt, he would buy and sell in all the markets of the world; but so would he be admitted to all the hells of the infernal region.

'By special grace, it has been revealed to me that it is the metaphorical mark of the beast – the love of money that would deliver a literal beast in the end of times. And the beast so sired would devour only those who carry the mark that begot it. Let those who carry the mark of the beast hear what the Holy Spirit says to the church.'

Chapter Two

In the western part of Sirama, six men lay in a Cimmerian darkness trying to come up with a foolproof or what they called a *kernel plan* on how to rob Sirama National Bank. They had been lying in this Cimmerian darkness for the past one-hour trying to fashion out a foolproof plan that would see them through the herculean task of robbing the bank with as little risk as would be left to the vagaries of fortune. The rendezvous was a large bunker under the house of the leader of the six-man robbery gang – Erince the Prince who normally host meetings of this nature. Lying inside the bunker, no man could see the other though it was then broad daylight. It was their policy not only to always meet in darkness, but as far as possible, carry out their robberies in the dark. Such arrangement secured their invisibility and invincibility. More importantly, darkness annihilates sight the most damnable traitor the Prince could perceive. According to him, sight was a detestable traitor that had betrayed mankind to the affliction of money – *the Lord Mammon* that makes a few people rich while the majority wallow in penury.

'Money – *the Lord Mammon,* may be a *common friend* to some people, but to many, it is an unjust god,' the prince always said; 'and it is *sight* that made money a god in the first place. *Sight* made money a god by turning the animal desires for food, clothing and shelter to human desires of greed, gluttony and pride. Animal desires for food, clothing and shelter do no harm. The lion kills only when it is hungry, and so a man seeks food only when he is hungry. The tiger is contented with its patch, and so a man is comfortable in his hut. The leopard is proud of its spots, and so a man is fine in his rags. But when desires become wanton, they become harmful. Desire is wanton if satisfying it leads to pride. Desire for a car, a castle and an aeroplane lead to pride when satisfied. It is sight that breeds desires whose satisfaction leads to pride. Men see cars and desire them. They see beautiful women and desire them. They go to any extent to get money to acquire the objects of their desires. Because money is the water that quenches the *desires, m*oney has turned into a god – an unjust god that makes a few people rich and the majority poor.'

The Prince seeing money as an unjust god that tyrannized mankind, set out to annihilate it. The best way he saw of annihilating money was by uprooting *sight* the traitor that betrayed mankind to the affliction of money. According to him, the root of all evil is not money, but *sight* that generates desires that triggers the quest for money. To uproot *sight*, he and his gang operated in the dark and lived as far as possible in the dark. They called themselves *the Cimmerian Brotherhood* and their bunker *Cimmeri*.

To the Cimmerian Brotherhood, life was a long tunnel of darkness with little glimmer of light. *This night*, was the only time reference in Cimmeri, not minding whether it was day or night. All the Cimmerians were members of the snake cult of Sirama. As a mark of honor and reverence for the snake, which they called the grandmaster, meetings in Cimmeri were completely in the nude and always had the snake in attendance.

Since the Cimmerians by common disposition banded together some seven years back, they held meetings according to the vagaries of necessity. The Prince, as leader of the Cimmerian brothers, arrived all meetings last.

In their Cimmerian world, they knew each other only by voice and recitation of their six cardinal principles: *devilish courage, total insulation against pity, brutalization of conscience, contempt for the organized society and its institutions, complete lack of faith in God*, and *derision for the law*. These principles, like catechism, were recited by each Cimmerian in all their meetings to reaffirm their desertion of obligation and ascertain the absence of a stranger in their midst.

Since the Cimmerians banded together in a *robbery cooperative* some years ago, all meetings were conducted with the Cimmerian brothers lying flat on their stomachs, their heads forming a small circle within and their legs forming a bigger circle without. Only the prince broke the harmony of this order. His legs flowed in where others' heads flowed out. They had a deadly oath of secrecy and allegiance binding them together. The oath though simple in utterance, was grim and skin-creeping in administration. Like recitation of the six cardinal principles, the oath of secrecy was administered at the end of the proceedings of each meeting by the Prince himself. Even while administering the oath, the prince remained prostrate.

When he recited a line of the oath, it would be repeated by the member taking the oath. It would go on like that from the first man to the last:

> When I promise, I promise
> Words of honor and binding
> No betrayal and cheating
> Only loyalty and valor
> Only affirming the greatness
> Of Cimmeri the valiant
> If my mind comes to vary
> If my heart comes to conflict
> With the words of my mouth
> Let my life turn to ashes
> By the tongue of the master.

The snake, usually a viper, would by invocation by the Prince be invited to verify the truth of the solemn oath taken by all the Cimmerian brothers with the exception of the Prince who was adjudged by other Cimmerians to be beyond reproach, if reproach meant betraying or deserting the Brotherhood. The snake always began its verification of loyalty by climbing the back of the man to the left of the Prince wriggling and patting him with its tail. While the snake was on a Cimmerian, the Prince would be chanting:

> Mighty of the mighties
> Dexterity master
> Crawler without limbs
> Sailor without sails,
> Of wisdom you are the giver,
> Of knowledge you are the fountain,
> Examine our ways,
> Examine our minds,
> Examine our hearts,
> If any be found betraying,
> If any be found revolting,
> Our master twirl round him,
> Our master strike him dead,
> Our master stay with the rest.

The snake finding no fault with a member, moved on to the next until it had gone full circle with only the Prince breaking the circle. Having moved round the Cimmerians, the snake would slip away to where it came from. If it had found any fault with any of them, it would have smitten him to death.

Even after a meeting, members of the Cimmerian Brotherhood still did not see each other as they evaporated back to their various residences in Sirama through tunnels connecting them with the bunker.

Now lying in their Cimmerian world, man after man from his prostrate position spoke, proposing what in his view would be the safest and foolproof plan of robbing the National Bank of Sirama. From his prostrate position, the voice of a Cimmerian sounded eerie and way out of this world.

The Prince spoke presently: 'Men of Cimmeri are we throwing in the towel on this important venture?' he asked, stretching out full length. 'I have listened to different speeches tonight; but none seems to rise above the ordinary security network of a *smash-and-grab outfit*. We have all failed to scare up a *master kernel plan* of how to successfully pre-empt the National Bank's security anticipation.' This was one thing about the Prince: big talk anchored on a ferocious intellect. 'Kokoto the Beans' proposal that we smash into the bank, grab and bolt, must fail, if the bank knows the first thing about security, and I bet you, it does.'

Kokoto the Beans was a little man with excessively long ears and a plateau head to match. Even for a midget, his legs were a pace too short. Before becoming a member of the Cimmerian Brotherhood, he was an accomplished and charismatic beggar of repute, if ever there was one. Passing by Rusumu motor park in Sirama, one could not resist dropping a coin or two into his begging bowl. The way he swirled the words in his awkward mouth before letting them out in a thrilling, musical tune, gave a lot of colour and perhaps even dignity to begging. And he had a thing about keeping good opening and closing hours. By 7.30 in the morning, he had thrown the doors of his *business premises* open, taking a rather respectable position by the side of the motor park. By 11 o'clock, he had closed shop and gone home believing that whatever was to be made that day had been made, since from experience, he seldom got anything towards noon or thereafter. He was on his way to stardom and wealth in begging when disaster struck. He lost his musical voice for no known reason. In place of the sweet nightingale voice sat a ragged, harsh voice that sent his *customers* packing. For days, he hung forlornly by the motor park watching the world drift by without a single soul looking his way; least give him something. Lacking in voice, which was his raw material, he was forced to close shop as a beggar and stay at home hungry and angry. How could people privy to his handicap and who in fact had been feeding him on account of that handicap desert him because he had no voice with which to thrill them? It was now clear to him that it was not his withered hand that he waved about that was on sale, but his sweet musical voice. He was smote with contempt for the world and swore vengeance though without the wherewithal of wreaking it. It was in this foul mood the Prince found him and took him to Cimmeri availing him the wherewithal of vengeance. But even in Cimmeri, he could only be said to merely make up the number, which the Prince for reasons best known to him had insisted to be six. If he had any use in Cimmeri, it did not go beyond running errands and giving worthless advice. Little wonder, he was nicknamed *Kokoto the Beans* by other Cimmerians.

'I have personally investigated and inspected the place,' the Prince went on; 'and I must tell you, I am highly impressed by what I have seen and learned. Whichever security firms fitted the various security gadgets in the bank certainly thought of everything in the book. None of the security devices leaves a loose end hanging which we can hold to break into the bank. As far as the National Bank is concerned, you don't dream of reaching a dime in the bank by the old catechism methods of smash-and-grab recommended by Kokoto the Beans. The bank for exception is not a smash-and-grab outfit, but a masterpiece in modern security engineering,' the Prince continued, his voice becoming intense. 'To start with perhaps what we all know, the bank has no single block in its construction. It is purely a steel affair from foundation to roof. The safes inside are the finest you can get anywhere in the world. The dogs are the best species of Alsatians. I will not be far from the truth if I call them hellhounds; and I bet you, I am not cutting it too fat. The doors are meltproof and smashproof; so also are the windows. There are no locks for you to fiddle with as the doors have automatic locks built into them. They slide close and open by means of a remote control in the custody of the manager. Mentioning the manager reminds me of the accountant and auditor in respect of another hard nut to crack in the bank: the bank safes. A safe does not open until the three combinations forming a lock-band have fallen into place. One of each of these combinations is with the manager, the accountant and the auditor. None of them knows the others' combinations. The three of them therefore have to come together to open a safe. The moment any of them twitch his combination into place, a small metal falls over it obscuring it from the view of the others. Tough, isn't it? Well, that's how it is, and more. The bank is electrified from head to bottom and the electrification is automatic. It comes on at 1900 hours and goes off at 700 hours exactly. While the current is on, any living thing that touches any metal in the bank with its bare body is a dead duck.'

'These guys have certainly thought of everything in the book,' Yomoyo *the owl* chuckled, exasperated and angered by the Prince's catalogue of the bank's security network. 'I bet even a bank in Pamsi the den of robbers will not think of going to this extent to secure itself,' he said anger making him pant.

Yomoyo was an intriguing and awesome member of the Brotherhood. Tall and broad featured, Yomoyo was smart in performance as in appearance. You could not fail to be impressed by the touch of professionalism wherever and whenever he struck. During robbery operations, he preferred leaving his victims dead than alive, possessed as he was by a child-like faith in the harmlessness of the dead. At the age of sixteen, he had left the regular society with a swaggering contempt to relieve in the underworld the choking bile conventional society inflicted on his psyche. He was capable of murder as he was of rape. He could commit matricide as coolly as he would kill a total stranger. Even with such a profile, for a long time, he shuddered at the memory of the first crime he committed against a nine-year old girl in his neighborhood. One night, after smoking marijuana and listening to heavy metal music in praise of the devil, he lured the girl away from their neighborhood under the pretext of buying her ice-cream from an ice-cream shop in some street across a cemetery. At the cemetery, on their way to the shop, he raped the girl, hacked her to death with a kitchen knife, ripped out her intestines and hung them on a tall mausoleum in the cemetery, and disappeared into the underworld where the Prince met him and took him to Cimmeri. So far, the Prince was yet to regret doing so.

'That's about it,' the Prince who not only had a brilliant mind, but a meticulous one said, his sharp and painstaking mind piecing the task on hand. He was a perfect hairsplitter. He spent all his time pondering on their robbery plans. He dissected each, piece by piece; examining each piece by turning it in his mind's palm to see if danger or trouble lurked somewhere. If it did, it was his duty to remove it. He never attempted a robbery until he had attempted it in his mind and it had succeeded without a finger pointing in his direction. He had a way of nailing his mind to a task and giving colour to his plans. This had earned him the unalloyed respect and loyalty of the Cimmerians. Throughout the seven years they had operated together from Cimmeri, they had remained what he said they were – shadows that could not be netted by *the dogs of the cabal* by which he meant the police.

To his fellow Cimmerians, perhaps nothing cast the Prince, who they also called the Wise Master, in such majestic splendor as his concoction of water Lethe – a mercuric substance said by the Prince to have been fetched by him from River Lethe which flowed somewhere in Cimmeri. When drank, this water produced amnesia the duration of which depended on the quantity taken. A little sip of the water induced amnesia lasting thirty days. The amnestic water of river Lethe was a happy antidote to the Cimmerians against the torment of conscience. It offers them an escape from the torment of memory to the bliss of forgetfulness. The moment it was taken, a thick curtain clammed down on the mind severing the past from the present and the future. The past went into oblivion for the period the effect of the water taken would last. The present and the future like a rewinding tape also moved into oblivion with the severed past. While the amnesia of water Lethe lasted, no robbery plan could be made or executed on account of loss of memory. For this reason, the water was only taken after chains of robbery operations whose proceeds would see them through the period of amnesia.

Unlike recitation of the six cardinal principles and oath-taking with the snake which were compulsory, the drinking of water Lethe was voluntary. The quantity a Cimmerian took, if he decided to drink the water, was also discretionary.

The Prince was led to concoct the water of river Lethe by his terror of memory and contempt for history – his own history in particular. *Memory* was to him the most damnable traitor of man after *sight*. After a man sees the comfort money the unjust god provides and the misery the lack of it breeds, what the eyes see is passed to *memory* for storage. In a way *memory* is a worse fiend than sight. His hatred of history arose from his understanding that history nurses *memory*. Undermining history therefore meant undermining *memory*. So, he attacked history. History he would say is a scroll of derelict accounts too abject for the attention of a man of destiny, and he saw himself as a man of destiny. As such a man, he perceived himself above the crippling facts of history and proceeded to appoint future eminence a sufficient cure for historical sentiments. Historians were to him one of those anomalies fantastic academia was capable of breeding. Without such allowance, he could not conceive the reasoning by which some men apply themselves to exhume the dirt of yesterday and others to patronize their ghoulish wares. Let historians and their masochistic audience like all donkeys continue to bray for the load of history. He, the prince with his fellow Cimmerians had enough guile to meet their malice and insane stupidity. He, the Prince and his fellow Cimmerians intended to go through life unmolested by history.

'I think we have come up against smart guys with a bloated sense of their self-preservation,' the voice of Jirimi the bat rang out of the depths of Cimmeri, his loose mind searching hopelessly for a suitable platform on which to come to terms with the task at hand – robbing the Sirama National Bank.

Jirimi in physique was a gaunt-looking man with sunken eyes that sometimes experienced difficulty seeing beyond his shadow. If physical appearance can furnish evidence of mental capacity, Jirimi's thwarted features were searing signatures of his mental dilemma. Essentially bird-witted and barren in imagination, Jirimi was incapable of thinking anything out to arrive at something with a semblance of a decision or plan of action. Any time he summoned his sterile faculties to conference, he found himself on a grinding plane pulverizing himself. Being so outmanoeuvred by congenital idiocy, he would rather have his hands lead him than his mind. No wonder he came to a lot of grief while running his one-man robbery outfit before throwing in with the Cimmerians. In Cimmeri, he was forced against himself to think before acting. He felt mentally harassed by the very prospects of the new dispensation. To think was painful enough. To process his thoughts into a plan of action was a tall order amounting to his mental torture. On this account, Jirimi resented the Prince with the passion of a zealot of the vegetative school. He was only persuaded to remain with the Cimmerian Brotherhood by a reflex liaison with the advantages of the Prince's rational methods over his impulsive methods. He felt the Prince's method of predicating action on a well thought out plan had first the advantage of acquainting him with the means and terrain of his robbery thereby making success a likely probability; and second, the advantage of withdrawing at the planning stage without attracting harm to himself, if success appeared an elusive prospect. On this score, his impulsive gravitation made allowance for only failure attended by appropriate retributive sanctions if caught by law. His last brush with the law on account of such failure, which earned him five ruinous years in jail, was enough counterweight to his difference with the thinking Prince. In Cimmeri, if only to satisfy the Prince who he feared rather than respected, he found himself like a dwarf mired in quicksand putting up a show of thinking whenever thinking was demanded. A wall of fire always separated him from the transcendent meditative Prince and he always shrank from it with the terror of Elijah* before the wiles of Jezebel. It was because of this pretense that he always cringed whenever the snake was on him during oath-taking, fearing the snake would strike him dead. However, since meetings where plans were thought out were like everything with the Cimmerian brothers held in the dark, his shows of being in the thinking process were quite unnecessary.

'What I know is that every human situation is simple, complex as it may seem,' said Makol. 'A thing is complex only because we don't know how it functions or its set-up. In this case, the Wise Master has acquainted us with the set-up of the National Bank. From what he said, the bank manager, the bank accountant and the auditor hold the key to a successful robbery of the National Bank. As the officiating priests in the bank's cultic set-up, they are the guys we have to deal with to reach the bank's vaults. On this score, fellow Cimmerians, we are thinking to something,' he concluded with earnest enthusiasm.

A prophet of God whom Jezebel the wife of Ahab king of Israel threatened to kill, forcing him to flee 1 Kings 19:1-8

Dismissed from the Dametan police force while serving in Suleni and sentenced to twenty-one years imprisonment for raping a fourteen-year-old girl about to be sent to a reformatory for delinquent behavior, Makol managed to break jail after spending only two years in detention. For three months, he stalked the backstreets of Suleni haunted by the fear of detection. The police force, his erstwhile constituency, became by the twist of events, his anxious nemesis against which he must deploy several devices to evade. But perhaps the most annoying backlash to his sense of community was that he was not only a fugitive from justice but from his consort as well. Ninatu, his live-in wife of four years would be the first person to report him to the police were he to yield to a passion for her society. He entertained no illusions about her sense of personal mortification over his breach of amorous ties. She had told him even before his conviction and sentence by the court how her name had been scandalized, her person insulted, and her womanhood betrayed by his pedophilic disposition. She had also told him how she had been suffered to listen to the gossip of two wanton women concerning his sexual indiscretion. One of the women who was their neighbor had, on sighting her, quipped loudly to her companion that monkeys did not learn to eat bananas until they had tasted beans. Knowing the scathing remark was meant for her ears rather than those of the companion, she had petulantly replied that vermin did not learn to feed on human blood until a soft body had been presented to them.

Throughout his trial, she was in court only once and that was the day of his conviction and sentence. On that day, he had, as had become his custom, surveyed the public gallery hoping against hope she would be in court. Though he longed to see her, he experienced a violent jolt when he saw her seated on the front row of the public gallery with those twinkling eyes of hers blazing beauty. Strange emotions swarmed over him like armed soldiers taking his mind captive. At last, when he was able to govern his emotions, a plea for forgiveness shot from his eyes towards her only to be chased away by a look of hate and revulsion on her face. He knew then he had with his hands murdered the love and squandered the goodwill he enjoyed from her. A stab of pain shot through his heart and his lips quivered visibly. He knew that so far as love was concerned, the sun had set for him. As there was no woman in his heart before her, there would be no woman in his heart after her. Other women would be there to satisfy his lust, but no other woman would be admitted into the sanctuary of his heart. He was at home with this brutal fact as he was at home with the hair padding his head. There was something about her that arrested the erotic in him, dispensing it in right measure to his total satisfaction. This thing, he was sure, he would not find in another woman. It was on this account he cursed the streak of character that made him sacrifice her love for the mess of pottage of a teenager.

When he broke jail, he was nearly lured home by his feelings for her. But such feelings were checked by memory of the revulsion on her face the last day he saw her and his morbid fear of going back to jail. He could stand the most unfriendly disposition of people towards him, but revulsion. Revulsion unhinged his very being, placing him on a revolving disc that drained all his self-esteem. Even with love as strong as his for Ninatu, he knew he could not put up with her revulsion. So, he drifted asunder, keeping to the backstreets of Suleni until he was able to filch enough money to take him to Sirama where he met the Prince who took him to Cimmeri. If the Prince had great respect for any Cimmerian's intellectual acumen and smart performance, it was Makol's.

'Given this set-up, we can cut the Gordian knot by kidnapping the three musketeers between us and the money in the vaults of the National Bank. Let them come to Cimmeri and assist us combat the present challenge,' Dikask another Cimmerian said swirling his fat tongue that would have found better accommodation in the mouth of a bull. He was a long-winded, arrogant loud-mouth and an oddity of some sort. A man of average height and average intelligence, he was an absurd looking man with a receding forehead and spouted lips that in a comic way underlined the recession of his forehead. He was in every respect a species fit for the theatre of the absurd and the laughable. He was a remarkably ugly man.

Before banding together with the Cimmerian Brotherhood, he led a strained life eking a living from various petty jobs that could barely support one stomach – his own. Today, he was a hawker of assorted wares; yesterday he was a barber; and the other day, he was a gardener. On the side, he applied his loose mind and light fingers to stealing whenever the opportunity presented itself. Of all his petty vocations, the one that most fascinated him was that of hawking. Being by nature a loose footed fellow, hawking tended more to his wandering spirit than any vocation could. But he was soon to discover that the vocation requires from its practitioners more than a dose of vagrancy. It requires a good dose of patience from anyone who means to prosper by it. This fact was drummed home to him by the annoying antics of patronizers of his wares, especially women. As it turned out, a woman put paid to his penchant for roaming the streets, hawking assorted wares.

One day, in the course of hawking his wares, a flimsy looking woman with a miserly front and a generous behind beckoned at him with strapping fingers that reminded him of the claws of a pigeon he stole in his neighborhood some years back while wandering listlessly in a football field. When he took the wares to her, for about three minutes, she hankered over all the articles in his wooden tray picking them one by one and examining them for hidden defects. She seemed quite undecided on what it was she actually wanted to buy. He stood looking at her, a wild storm of anger gradually building up in his beady eyes as she seemed to find defect with every item from the various shades of expression that played guest to her shriveled face. Then her eyes lit up, gleaming like chips of emerald in the sun. She seemed to have lighted upon what she wanted. His clouded face went a shade brighter.

She picked up a toy car; placed it on the palm of her left hand and flapped it off from the rear. The toy skidded off her palm and nose-dived towards the dusty ground. He made a dive for it and in the process tripped over the wooden tray containing his wares. It tumbled over spilling his articles all over the place. His frayed nerves were totally deranged. With bile nearly choking him, he managed to pack the articles back into the wooden tray and asked with a fell note in his voice, 'which item do you actually want to buy, madam?'

'None that I can see in your cheap wares,' she replied snobbishly.

'Bitch, misfortune of a bastard,' he snorted angered beyond tolerance limits. 'You won't buy anything and indeed have no money to buy anything, yet you wasted my time and soiled my goods with your sluttish association and bitchy prevarication. I invoke the curse of all the damn gods of your blasted tribe upon your blighted life,' he blared, the fingers of his left hand fanned out in an abusive gesture. His articles of trade were between him and the woman. As he grew more abusive and drew nearer her, she suddenly spat into his face, picked the wooden tray containing his articles of trade and flung it into the bush.

Quite strangely, he did not for a moment shut his eyes though her spittle had actually fallen into his right eye. Seeing what the woman had done, coupled with her annoying antecedents, he jumped at her his muscular hands reaching out for her throat.

The agility he sprang and the fact that the woman expected an attack by him to be checked by her saliva in his eyes, made it impossible for her to avoid or even reduce the impact of his attack. His huge hands swallowed up her fragile neck and squeezed, all the biceps and sinews in them, rippling with excitement of the taunted. Her tongue fell out, her eyes rolled into a whitish shade and her body sagged like the lilies of the field before the wind.

The neighborhood was particularly deserted at the hour of these goings-on by its inhabitants who had all proceeded to their various vocations. By the time two boys about sixteen and eighteen were attracted to the scene, the woman was already dead. When Dikask observed their approach, he propped up the body of the dead woman against his own in the manner of a sick person being lugged along by an attending relation. As he moved stealthily, he occasionally threw a furtive glance over his shoulders to ascertain how matters stood between him and the obtrusive boys.

The boys, observing in the duo a relationship of a friendly complexion rather than one of a hostile character they had intuitively presumed, slung away in an opposite direction. Dikask having ascertained by his furtive glances the withering of danger, laid the dead woman across the path and fled like the children of Israel before the army of Ai.*　In the face of capital danger, his mind took no thought of his wares.

Though the murder of this woman was his first, he experienced no regrets killing her. He felt she was by all showing a doomed fatalist keeping a date with her pale destiny, and he was merely the available means her fatal star chose to shine. By all account, he was only a predetermined agent of an evil fate. However, the murder of the woman marked the end of his life as a toyman, and indeed as a hawker of any type of wares. In quick succession, he took to several vocations lacing them with thievery until the Prince met him and took him to Cimmeri.

A small city east of Bethel whose army defeated the Israelites army on account of Achan's sin. By their defeat the Israelites were forced to flee. Joshua 7:1-15.

Chapter Three

Josira, a lady of a certain age, for the third time, peered at herself in the wall mirror in her one-room apartment and seemed quite thrown by what she was seeing. Could she be the middle-aged woman with a paling skin and faded features staring back at her?

'Oh God, what is happening to me?' she asked of no one. She turned her back on the mirror and took a cursory survey of her little room. It appeared to her the room had joined her somber appearance in a derisive celebration of her parlous state. To her right stood her CD player jetting a melodious tune which, but for her melancholy, would have tended exquisitely to her musical taste. Now, where the music was gay, she read jest into it, and where it pulsated to a monotone, she read dirge into it. She switched off the player and presented herself once again before the mirror, perhaps in a final resolve to separate a phantom from her real self. She started by examining her eyelashes; they were not as thick and bewitching as they were in her first flush. Turning to the eyelids, she discovered that tinctures, like fugitive snoopers, had crept under the lower lids. As for her pupils, they had lost some of their spark and feminine lure. Though her hair still retained its bloomy character, she seemed to think it might not hold out against her general debasement for long. She took measured steps towards the door, and felt her steps had lost their youthful spring of a sweet-twenty. Suddenly feeling old and beaten, she flung herself on her bed and cried herself to a fitful sleep.

When she woke up, she confronted the blonde beast preying on her with this simple logic: Since her worn features were the result of men's sexual abuse and lack of money, not from the natural process of aging, men should provide the money to restore her to her prime shot. Money to her was *the healing water of River Jordan*. It was the only thing she needed to turn her situation around. With the *healing water of River Jordan,* the withering flower can become robust again. Lack of money was the drought withering her. Money was *the holy water of River Jordan that will cure her of the leprosy of poverty*. Men were the Jordan, the source of *the holy water*. So, she would have to device means of getting men sprinkle their water on her.

Chapter Four

'Give your widow's mite,' Pastor Gojang cried, striding north and south before his flock inside his church newly founded according to divine order and called *Give Christ the Glory Church* – GCGC. Before Pastor Gojang acquired the building for the Godly purpose of Christ ministration, the same building with a grove-like appearance had served the worldly purposes of beer parlour, restaurant and brothel in that order. Whenever it changed purpose, structural alterations in the form of partitions were effected in tune with every purpose. In tune with the structural alterations, paints of different colours adorned the building in a chameleonic fashion. However, except for Pastor Gojang who took time and expense to have the old paint washed before repainting, previous occupants of the building had simply applied their own paint on the building treating the former paint more like a whitewash. The result was that loud colour paints resisted submergence under faint colour paints thereby producing in effect variegated colours like a Buddhist scroll.*

It was in this colour crisis Gojang bought the building. He saw or thought he saw in the colour crisis, tell-tale signs of the sordid affairs

---

* *A Buddhist parchment of variegated colours depicting torments in hell.*

that once took place in the building and decided to erase all signs that forebode ill for his purpose of winning souls for the hereafter. His effort in this regard bequeathed on the building a dignified aspect that beseemed its Godly purpose.

'The widow's mite; that is what you should bring to the house of the lord Yahweh,' Pastor Gojang repeated again, reaching for the umpteen time for his handkerchief that spent more time in transit than in either his pocket or face. 'And I hope you all know what this means. Some of you without divine understanding I believe are wont to give literal interpretation to the widow's mite with all its absurdities and annoyance to the lord Yahweh: The interpretation that widow's mite means nothing is too small to be given to God. Brethren, such interpretation is absurd and mischievous. Speaking according to divine inspiration, widow's mite means widow's might. It means giving God all that one has, not the base, the rotten or the despised of one's possessions. The widow from whom the expression got its popularity had nothing but the farthing she gave to God. Therefore, she gave all she had. So likewise, if three cars, two houses, five shoes or whatever, are your possessions, you must give all to the Lord Yahweh to be deserving of giving your widow's mite. This, brethren, is what the scripture is saying regarding the giving of one's widow's mite,' he said, expanding his chest in tune with the expanding spiritual inspiration in him.

'The scriptures abound with instances of men and women of God who gave their widow's mite,' he pursued, his eyes on a man he had observed parking a Mercedes 600 popularly called *the Beast* to enter the church. The beast might be hated in heaven, Pastor Gojang would not mind having this kind of beast around him on earth. The man from his appearance was money in flesh and blood. Such a man as he was one after Pastor Gojang's heart and he was already spreading his net towards him.

'Is it king David that would not build the house of the Lord on gifted land, or the woman that poured expensive oil on Jesus' feet, or Abel that took his fattest lamb to the Lord of host, or Abraham that was ready to sacrifice his only begotten son? All these men, we are told by the scriptures, exceedingly pleased God, and he blessed them for giving their widow's mite. What was more, he gave them more than the miserly hunks to whom mammon is a god. Talking about hunks, reminds me of the rich fool who without giving his widow's mite, lauded himself with such buffoonery of rest and pleasure that made the Lord take his life that night. Talk of an overfed fly tearing its protruding stomach with its own legs! What of the young and haughty rich man who prided himself as an observer of the laws of Moses from youth, but woefully failed the litmus test of foregoing all he had before marching towards paradise with Christ. By the words of his mouth, he loved Christ all right. But his love did not go near his pocket. Therefore, when Jesus drew it towards his pocket, he, like the deceitful jade* he was, sank in the trial. My brethren, wretched and crooketh is that love that stops short of the pocket. Our man, the young rich man, proved once more like all rich men, too fat for the eye of the needle. The question here is, how many of us have spread themselves so thin as to pass through the eye of the needle? How many? That is the question we have to answer and fast too.' He paused for them to size themselves against the Biblical heavenly thoroughfare then continued rather sententiously; 'many of us here look so fat that were the eye of the needle to be enlarged by divine will to admit two camels, they will still turn up too fat to enter it. Yes! such is the surfeit and obesity of today that we are irredeemably lost to heaven. We preachers, the divinely ordained shepherds of the lost sheep, are not listened to by sheep committed to straying further into the wilderness. Even so, we shall not tire. I, Pastor Gojang, for one, will not tire. I will continue to plead with the sheep to turn back and head home.

'As many as hear my voice and hearken shall be Lazarus in kingdom come. As many as refused, will be the rich man in hell the house of fire and brimstone. Yes!' he continued in an

---

A worthless horse, which cannot be relied on in any horse race. See Shakespeare's Julius Caesar Act 4 scene II.

apparent rare access to divine insight. 'On a sober reflection and reading between the lines, I have come to the irresistible conclusion Lazarus was so poor because he never took thought to pile money down here on earth where termites and rats would eat into, but up there in heaven where neither rats nor termites shall near. The rich man on the contrary was busy piling his own here on earth and was the worse for it in heaven. Thus, while Lazarus was spreading himself thin in preparation to passing through the eye of the needle, the rich man was heaping himself too fat in preparation to not entering it. Men, be wise in spiritual matters as you are wise in material things,' he counseled, and engaged the eyes of *the big cheese* who inwardly flinched from his boring and pecking eyes.

'Many of you would without experiencing any difficulty of thinking, stash away money in Swiss banks where it would be temporarily safe, but would not likewise think of sending some to heaven where it would be permanently safe, and what is more, where your future lies! He is a wise soldier who insists his salaries be paid to his wife and children at home rather than to him in the battlefield where death stalks him with the regularity of a flying column. Likewise, he is a foolish soldier who has his paid to him in the battlefield only to leave it to the enemy when the darts of war claim him,' he said in such abject tone that some of his flock thought he would rather their salaries were paid direct to the church than to them. 'My brethren, be wise soldiers and never feel it too late to be a wise soldier if you have been a foolish one all your life. The good Lord is ever merciful and ready to forgive brethren,' he spoke in a low, penetrating tone as if tearing open the hearts of his flock to lodge these words. 'Forgiveness! That is the great thing that makes all the difference between the Christian God and other gods. Our God is ever so reasonable and merciful that he can forgive and forget the most heinous of deeds in the face of humility and repentance. That is the staying quality of our God that has made him keep faith with humanity through the ages and generations. Therefore, the politician who looted the national treasury yesterday can be forgiven today if only he repents of his sins and turns to God. So also the thief and the armed robber that have fallen outside the pale of human kindness by killing to be rich, if only they will repent, turn to this God and receive not only his forgiveness, but his blessings as well. After all, on the day of judgment, the question will not be whether one had sinned, but whether he had repented of his sins. That will be the crucial test my brethren: repentance. Because all have sinned through our first parents Adam and Eve, and there is no great or small sin. Sin is sin. What then reconciles man to God is repentance, which is by faith. But faith we know is not enough. It must be backed up by works, the greatest of which is the giving of one's widow's mite. In point of fact and spirituality, giving of widow's mite has been counted one of the seven works of spiritual mercy, while miserliness is one of the seven deadly sins. He that has ears to hear, let him hear,' he said in that varied tone that attends conclusions of great sermons. He took his seat on the pulpit.

The service leader stood up to announce it was time for church offering. Again, the eyes of Pastor Gojang strayed to the opulent man. 'Has the rat bitten the bait?' he wondered despairingly.

Chapter Five

The finer details of carrying out *operation outsmart the jackal* as the Cimmerians dubbed their epoch-making robbery of Sirama National Bank, were supplied by the Prince. The Prince was the fifth child of a family of seven children in the small town of Famla in Expero a former colony of England. As a child, the Prince, frail and often sick for a good part of his childhood and early adolescence, hung between life and death. But by some miracle, he survived childhood and adolescence to adulthood shedding off incessant sickness, but retaining frailty of aspect. He was a man of extraordinary intelligence, possessing a razor-sharp mind. In character, however, he was coarse and rude. His parents were descendants of the Maare clan and were quite poor even by Famla's town standards, which were very low.

The Prince grew up to hold his father, a devout Christian, responsible for their poverty. And that was how his mind worked. He subjected human situations to the righteous spectacle of a pragmatist and proceeded to give judgment according to what he perceived to be human failure. Rarely did he assign providence to the fortunes of men. As for the hand of God in the affairs of men determining who shall be rich and who shall be poor according to the Islamic faith of his mother, he did not see it even as a teenager. And if nature had any *way* about it according to the

Taoist literature he had read more than anything else, he considered it his duty to resist such *way* of nature as tended to his embarrassment through a blighted existence. He evaluated circumstances and happenings drawing only from the material world he could see, and it was one he should grab whatever tends to his comfort with the only consideration and care that he was not caught taking it. If he had any conscience, he did not show it. From his conduct and behavior in childhood, he showed himself capable of doing anything mean for financial gain without the least misgivings. If his action brought shame to his parents, so much the better for them. Having insured his poverty, they could not but occasionally pay the premiums. It was his office to keep reminding them of their uncelebrated lives through such acts as affected them in his culpability. Whenever he saw his father reading the Bible in front of the house, he swore murder as he contemptuously hissed at him. 'What a bone-idle fellow,' he would grumble murderously. It beat his understanding and imagination how a man could go through life praying to a God he could not see and who could not make up for his shortcoming of being invisible by making his existence felt through a comfortable life for his worshippers. Such a *wonderful* God surely deserved only his contempt, and that equally went for his abject worshippers. In some way, it could be said the poverty of his parents set him on the warpath with conventional religion, and by extension, society. His parents' lack of money also seemed to make him have an unusual love for money. Obsessed with money, he came to see it as a god. But it was an unjust god that favoured a few people leaving the majority in poverty. He was to later make it his messianic mission to save mankind from the unjust god money was by taking them to Cimmeri where they would no longer see the comforts money provided and where they would drink water Lethe to forget the comforts of money they had seen or indeed enjoyed.

The day he was born, even his parents sensed that something more sinister than their poverty has come into the family. It was an uncanny feeling they could not account for. There were no peculiar features on the Prince setting him out as an evil child except that he had six fingers and paraded a snub nose. Otherwise, he was a normal child. Perhaps, what gave rise to their feeling were the bats that kept rustling in and out of the dongo tree behind their house on the day he was born and their other children who fell sick that day as if protesting his coming into their world. The Prince himself did not help matters with the unnatural smile that hung on his lips instead of the cry expected of a child just coming into the world. He did not cry in protest of coming into the world, but like the proverbial Cheshire cat, he smiled at the world he was coming to rape and murder, leaving the crying to his siblings.

As he warmed his way through childhood to adolescence and manhood, one thing spoke eloquently for him: his great capacity for observation and a towering intellect. When these qualities began to impress themselves on his parents, they were elated. This, perhaps, was the child that would bear the family's bell; the child that was not a chip of the old block; for they were anything but brilliant, and all their children before the Prince had only demonstrated high capacity for idiocy and aggravated imbecility. But here was the Prince with a towering and imposing intellect set to change all that. And true to their expectation, he did change all that, but not in the light they thought he would, but in the darkness they did not dream of.

As a child of eleven, he was already stunned by the destitution of his family, which insulted and taunted the dignity of man. His family could not have breakfast, though they fasted more than anybody having not eaten the previous night. The wretched meal that passed for their breakfast and dinner rolled into lunch was, to use his words, bound for the pigs but steered towards them by poverty. He had only two shirts and only one trouser that had lost its seat; the shirts covered with holes and patches. He had neither shoes nor a sweater to protect him from the cold during harmattan. During severe harmattan periods, he and his brothers and sisters stayed indoors to keep warmth by the fire burning in the mighty hearth inside their courtyard. His bitterness and anger against his father who he blamed for his wretched circumstances turned into a murderous rage when he started going to the secondary school in Famla, which was far from his home. He and his siblings had to trek five kilometers barefooted, and often on empty stomachs to get to the school. As gravel pinched their bare feet supporting flagging bodies, children better circumstanced sped past them on bicycles and with shoes on their feet. To him, it was luxury to have shoes. The child that had shoes and was riding a bicycle was living a life in grandiose jest of his own.

In school, he found most advantaged children trying to put a distance between him and them. He felt sick and vengeful. Even some of the teachers did not make him feel he belonged. Not that any teacher or student had ever given voice to his low opinion of him and his poor circumstances, but their actions and attitudes towards him tormented him more than words would have. Since they avoided him, he avoided them bidding his time to hit out at anybody that came within his range.

The first person to come within his range was Sil his younger brother of three. Wherever and however he got the money, he got it and bought a small radio, he carried about listening to what was happening around the world and how he would fit himself into it. Already, he was fast losing patience with the narrow and blighted world of his home and neighbourhood and wanted out. He felt he had put up with this world for too long and would soon leave it without the courtesy of an excuse. Towards this end, he had left school and banded together with a gang of boys in Famla known as the *Hell-benders* whose main occupation was robbery and occasional gang-rape whenever any woman was unfortunate to run into them in isolation.

Only his mother protested when he left school. As far as his father was concerned, he was entitled to his action, having told him to his face, what an affront he was to humanity for failing to lift his family to human standards. The mother on that occasion was aghast and quite thrown seeing the Prince and hearing the horrifying words he spat out with such verbal violence and savagery that hardly was to be expected of a boy his age. The father merely slumped his head, chewing his lower lips. From that day, he gave up on the Prince, consigning him to the devil. If a child that young could look at his father, or for that matter any adult, and accuse him to his face of failing humanity, then such a child was beyond redemption, beyond all hope of correction by scolding him when he stole as the Prince did and was reprimanded by him; because in such a child resides the devil himself – the king of armed robbers and of all evil. It was then to the father not the Prince that spoke, but the devil inside him.

When the Prince returned home one day to collect his radio, which he had somehow forgotten at home, he found it lying on the ground in their courtyard where Sil his younger brother had dropped it. He picked it up and switched it on, but there was no sound coming from it. It was then he thundered, and jinn, as his mother later lamented, reared his head threatening to come out of him stark naked in all his crudities and monstrosities. His eyes shone with the freedom and dignity of the wild beast. The mouth that spoke and the eyes that glared merged into a decisive and crushing evil.

'Who touched my radio?' he asked, completely slate-loose.

His mother cooking in the kitchen spoke, 'It was Sil. I hope he has not spoiled it for you?'

'Who?' he yelled, his tiny voice carrying only that quantity of menace it could accommodate leaving the rest to his hands. 'Sil!' he shouted pouncing on the boy who stood not too far away from him. Before their mother could come out of the kitchen in response to Sil's yells for help, the Prince had turned Sil upside down and knocked his head on the ground. Their mother arrived the spot to find only the lifeless body of Sil lying on the ground with the Prince on the run with the keys to streets he had always wanted to be on. He never set his foot into his father's home again.

Chapter Six

Josira felt like being split on a rock. One moment, she was denouncing her past and the next moment she was embracing it as the only available route to her rejuvenation. Anybody in her position had the right to mourn.

She was a pair of a set of twins of a Sulenian family. As her twin brother Lonkoj was born with an Oedipus complex, she was born with an Electra complex; and as he was obsessed with money, she was possessed by it. She and her brother were the only children of their parents. While they were both light skinned, she was lighter than her brother. Much of the education she had, was acquired from her father Mimono whose only virtue was his taking time to teach her how to read and write in the English language and also acquainting her with general knowledge of subjects of education he knew.

She was deflowered by her father Mimono at the age of fourteen. It happened one night when her mother Mekelin a devout Christian had gone for an all-night revival prayer in church, and Lonkoj had for the three days preceding the incestuous day, travelled to Okunta a nearby small town to help his uncle in his farm. She and her father Mimono were the only two living souls in the house the day it happened.

Three days after the event, Mekelin a normally healthy woman, died of high fever. Lonkoj the closest person to her in the family was the first to know her demise. Having been sick for the past two days, he had early in the morning of the third day, gone to her bed to see how she was getting on only to find her dead. It was his lamentation that brought both Josira and Mimono to her bedside.

Mimono to whom Mekelin was not more than a meal ticket mourned her only for that reason. Having come to rely on her for his upkeep and that of their two children, he was grieved as to how future sustenance was to come. Mekelin, enterprising and possessed by an ancient sense of responsibility, like mother hen always scratched up something for the family to feed on. If she was not plaiting a woman's head, she was selling firewood all in a bid to keep the family going. Whatever she got from her various economic ventures, went up in the up-keep of the family as Mimono never got round to any paying vocation beneficial to the family. On the few occasions he had money, he blew it up in the beer parlor. The death of Mekelin therefore placed before him than anything would have done his failure as a breadwinner for his family. But that was all it did. It did not change him from being an idler to a go-getter.

In the morning of her death, Mimono went to dig Mekelin's grave in the public cemetery. With their two children looking on, he took her corpse in the clothes she died in and dumped it inside the grave. He pushed the dug soil over her and left with Lonkoj crying and screaming. He never forgave Mimono for his mother's death; for he knew her death was caused by him. As for Josira, the same hatred he bore Mimono, he nursed for her by reason of the same complicity in their mother's death. For days, he went to weep by his mother's graveside.

One day, tormented by an obsessive desire to see her again, he clawed and tore at the loose earth of the grave, exhuming her dead body. The stench that assailed his nostrils made him sick and dizzy. From the cemetery, he did not go back home, but strode away, a forsaken child with only the keys to the streets in his hands.

After her mother's death, she became the consort of her father until she met Kargan a young man who lived in the neighborhood. Kargan appeared to have more money than her father and was livelier and more innovative in what he called *the moaning game* than her father who was losing steam on account of age. She was faced with the task of breaking with a debauched father who was becoming increasingly violent in his jealousy.

'Hold your horses!' Mimono cried, barricading her from going out of their one-room apartment on the day that turned out their last together. He had sat on their sleeping mattress in their room with scarcely enough space to swing a cat watching her preparing to go out to where, only

God knew, and to come back when, only God knew. 'You know as a daughter you are not supposed to be showing total disrespect to your father,' he stormed at her.

'Ha! ha! ha!'

'Josira!'

'As a father are you supposed to be sleeping with me?'

'But, Josira you know that is no good way to talk to your father. At least I slept with your mother to beget you.'

'And so you must sleep with me? Shameless old he-goat!'

'Josira, are you sure you are well?'

'Suck your stinking, reddish arse, rotten old beans!'

'But you haven't complained much before now. I took it that you didn't mind.'

'If I don't mind, shouldn't you as a responsible father? Does my irresponsibility entitle you to irresponsibility? Answer me cowhead!'

'Josira!'

'Fuck your stinking yellow arse!'she screamed as she shoved him violently sideways and fled the house for good.

Mimono fell on his back and vowed not to rise up until she comes back to raise him whenever that would be. From where he lay, his mind went back to the day she was born and how she had been close to him. He could remember how his wife was strongly resentful of her unsettling attachment to him and her total detachment from her, which sometimes bordered on hostility. Likewise, he could remember Lonkoj's preference for his mother over him with similar hostility towards him. His mind came down to the day he deflowered Josira and stayed there for quite sometimes reliving and relishing every moment of that first night. Then it descended unwillingly to when she started losing interest in their incestuous romance even before Kargan came into the scene. Finally, it stepped down sluggishly to Kargan's eruption on the scene, which event has led to his lying on the floor of their room.

Beginning with the day she was born, she was born into an empty house without food and without love. It was one quarrel and fight after the other between him and his wife, and he was often the cause of most quarrels and fights. Educated though he was, he won no trophy from his education. Against all his manifest faults, he found Josira growing up to like him more than her mother. This remained the case even after she became old enough to suspect his responsibility for the family's poor circumstances. So close was she to him that she could only go to sleep with him. This continued long after she had entered her age of puberty; and it was in her puberty age of fourteen it happened. One night when he returned home drunk to the hilt, he found her lying faced-up without a stitch on, fast asleep. The wrapper she went to sleep in had fallen off in the course of sleep. Beside him and her, no one else was at home. He stood on the doorway like the vicar of incubus in a toga of lechery, his eyes taking in all the lewd details of her naked form. Lust snarled at him and erotic excitement stirring up in him growled at the tiny cord of reason restraining his tumble over the precipice. Strange emotions invaded any sanity still in him. He was no Joseph. On the contrary, he was a hellbender and a square of the dames swaying between the loose and the indecent. The tenuous ligature of restrain held for only a moment against his lust's determined hauling. It snapped plunging him with a long leash of moral predicament into her bosom.

After the deed was done, he felt dirty within and wretched without. By the stroke of the act, he counted himself worthy of the most severe denigration among the vilest scum to ever walk the earth. He saw himself as a counterfeit being with a moral crisis threatening to disjoin filial harmony. For one sickening moment, he felt his entire being arrested by the monstrous implications and dire consequences of the act. All societal strictures and established filial sentiments came swooping down on him like a host of hungry locusts. His body shook and a tormented cry of anguish escaped his lips.

For Josira, her feelings after the act were quite opposite to those of Mimono. The gratification of her body was the gratification of her mind. Where Mimono felt dirty, she felt clean;

where he felt empty, she felt full. Erotic excitement hitherto beyond her wildest imagination, Mimono had placed before her. She was not beyond suspicion of confusing Mimono's parental care with his ministration to her sexual desires. Where a daughter would demand filial love from her father, she demanded erotic love from Mimono. Having no moral scruples at this point of the twist in filial relationship, there was no moral leash on her neck for him to secure her to the moral tree. He that had a leash was like a goat that could not tie itself to the moral tree. His unease about their drift into incestuous relationship was misunderstood by her and ascribed to alien worries. When the cry of anguish escaped his lips after their first romp, she thought he was physically sick and attended to him with a soothing balm which led to their rolling in the sack for the second time that night. When she started growing a moral leash, that of Mimono had come off. She that had the leash, like a goat, was unable to tie herself to the moral tree until Kargan burst into the scene.

Kargan was a Tamsa boy living in the same neighborhood with Josira and Mimono. Long before he started rooting for her, he had placed her and Mimono under observation and seemed not to like what he was seeing. Apparently Josira looked like a daughter to Mimono. But he could see an intimate relationship that seemed to carry them out of the filial relationship of father and daughter to the amorous relationship of husband and wife. He made it his business to find out exactly what was between the old man and the beautiful young lady; after all, he had made other things much more trifling the concern of his life. He started stalking them wherever they went. What he found out filled his mind with disgust for Josira and contempt for Mimono. Crouching behind their window one evening, he heard Josira saying, 'daddy what will you eat?' to which Mimono grunted that anything would do for him as there was not much to choose from.

'So, he is her father as I have suspected,' Kargan muttered, letting out a faint whistle of surprise, which, fortunately for him, could not be picked up by Mimono's good ears because it coincided with Josira telling Mimono to sit up and turn an honest penny for once in his idle life.

'But wait boy,' he counseled himself. 'Because she called him *daddy* doesn't necessarily mean he is her father for sure. With the crazy sweet names cooed everywhere in the kingdom of the flesh, *daddy* no longer needs to refer to a biological father. It could be the call-name for a lover.'

But what followed later completely put him in the clear concerning the biological relationship between Mimono and Josira.

Josira and Mimono having finished eating what Josira had prepared, Mimono said, 'sweetheart, you are really sweet and I hope you also find me sweet.'

'As bitter leaf, yes,' she said, drawing her lips in a sneer.

'Somehow, I can't account for the vacillation of your affection for me,' he said bitterly, his brow creasing to a forlorn aspect. 'Time was when you used to dote on me like a groom before the call of the chaplain.'

'Such time as you gloat over, I cringe to remember as days of my wanton folly, when I supposed the reed of the degenerate that begot me could also be the snout that will irrigate my lower regions. The folly of it now sometimes overwhelms me,' she said, the sneer on her face exploding to wreak havoc on her facial symmetry.

'Josira!'.

'Yes, and I suppose it is time you wake up to the reality of your folly before Old Nick claims your demented soul for his lower regions; though on that eventuality, my own lower region would have won a poetic justice of some sort.'

'Josira, you have played me fast and loose; engaging me while I was yet reluctant and disengaging me when I have gone wino on your virginal honey,' Mimono said tearfully, his face besieged by a nameless fear. 'Like the daughters of Lot,* you exploited my libidinal foibles only to

---

* *The two daughter of Lot who while living alone with their father in a cave in a mountain got him drunk and slept with him to perpetuates their family lineage: Genesis 19:30-38.*

mock me on the morrow. Like Delilah,* you engaged my fancy only to betray me to the Philistines.'

'Soto!' she blared, perceiving him in a hazy vision that sometimes reduced him to a mere dot on a distant surface and sometimes drew him near to explode him to smithereens. 'The philistines you have always carried in your libido, and I count it an act of unmerited divine favor they have not claimed your debauched soul before now,' she said in a flush of comic analogy.

Kargan did not wait to hear more. For the first time, he came close to appreciating what people meant when they talked of immorality. The following day he was up in arms against Mimono. He thought it a crime even against his own standards to stand by watching a demented man like Mimono desecrating a youthful gem like Josira. He would free her from Mimono's 'satanic' clutches for his own gratification. To this end, he continued stalking them like a shadow wherever they went until one afternoon he found Josira alone and confronted her with his messianic mission. She was taken aback, less by the proposition, as by the rude flush it was presented. As it turned out, he was the first young man to accost her with the gospel of love. For this, she admired him. The line between admiration and infatuation being tenuous,

---

A woman with whom Samson a Nazirite from birth and a strong man of Israel who rescued the Israelites from the subjugation of the Philistines fell in love and who betrayed him to the Philistines. Judges 14:1-20.

Kargan who had been in the game for long, using money as bait, was able to clear it with little effort. Before Mimono knew what was happening, Josira was beside herself in fantasies with Kargan. It was Kargan sure of his hold on Josira's heart and Mimono's shaky hold that carried the news to Mimono. Like a protégé of Hathor – the Egyptian goddess of love, music and dancing, he came one evening when he knew Mimono would be home, spouting love the Indian fashion: in songs and dances. Mimono listened wondering which lunatic was singing and dancing in the direction of his house. Kargan did not let him wonder long as he burst into their room in full feathers, pounced on Josira and pulled her up to dance with him. Mimono was struck dumb and paralyzed for a minute or so before he could assemble his wits and respond to Kargan's effrontery. By the time he was about responding, Josira like Nataraja the dancing siva in Hindu mythology was already singing and dancing with Kargan. He was again sent into another round of paralysis. By the time he came out of it, Kargan was gone. From that day, he knew the question of Josira leaving him was merely one of time as her relationship with Kargan heat up cooling off hers with him.

'What a rat, what a ...goof, what a... Jack nasty, what a.... Oh God of a boy?' Mimono cried from where he lay. 'How can the father of such a son not come to misgivings about his true parentage?'

Well, whatever happened, he was not leaving the floor until Josira comes back and lift him out of the sorrow she had plunged him. Otherwise, he was determined to remain where he was and die there. He kept this vow.

Two days later, he was still on the floor of their room refusing to stand up and attend to himself. When hunger cast the shadow of death over him, he denounced death thus: 'Death, whose child are you? You are neither the child of God nor that of man. Even the old enemy has disowned you. Death, you are a homeless bastard and I defy you to do your worst.' When his throat began to rattle like a broken bucket, he reached for his long knife and confronted death once more. 'Death, are you a thing to be feared as such? What good has wretched life bestowed on me to warrant my fear of you?'

Then in conspiratorial tones, he whispered to his haunting memory of Kargan, 'boy, let me tell you something. Life is but a revolving cycle of nemesis. You do me in today saving your miserable soul only for the morrow of your nemesis. Imp, I assure you it will light upon you with the swiftness of a cat your inert mind took no thought of. Mmm... Boy, life is but a dismal failure of comedy. When I was your age, it held a special appeal to me. It was a privilege to be born. So, it seems to all youth. But that life is an empty promise, we all soon discover. Happiness is not the due of the sane, but the special privilege of the insane. Why? Because only the insane can see and live out the ultimate truth: that all thought is ill, all strife is waste and all hope is vain. While it lasted, I enjoyed my lunacy. But you pushed me down to the hold of sanity and I cannot face the gloom that there is purpose and sense in life. Why shouldn't I embrace the ultimate forgetfulness?' Saying this, he reached for his genitals and neatly severed them off, then sank his teeth into the loose earth that was the floor of their room to stifle the screams that came welling from the innermost pit of his being. It was in that position he died and tumbled down in a grotesque tableau.

Chapter Seven

Pastor Gojang carrying a slim figure, suave in appearance and mannerism looked every inch a minister of God ordained in accordance with divine grace and calling. His church, Give Christ the Glory Church, was situated towards the tail end of Dunsal street in Sirama. When he founded the church, he thought it was only a matter of time for the money, which he needed more than anything in life, to start trickling in; then pouring in. However, six years after founding the church, he was still riding the weather-beaten car he was riding before founding the church and his bank account was yet to have the funds he had expected. Doubt began to cloud his optimism. But he would not accept he was a gone coon in the Christ ministry business, though for him and his Give Christ the Glory Church, it has been so much cry with little wool, so far as money was concerned.

As a man of God, he had a conflicting vision of money. It was a beast his flock must spurn, but *holy water* they should bring to the church. Each time he checked his bank account and saw it close to the red line, his heart took a frightening leap down. When he drove the boneshaker he called his car, he was driven to despair. When the rattletrap stopped on the road and coughed like an old woman afflicted by influenza, he had a sinking feeling. There were also his dresses and his wife's which were beginning to show signs of fatigue and might soon give in to wear and tear. Not that on such occasion he would blame them. No, he wouldn't. It would be a mark of ingratitude to do so. The spirit of Christ in him would not permit that.

He had to do something to stem his gradual drift to an undesirable union with the rats of his church. But what was he to do? Should he again invite Pastor Wollia to preach in his church on the need to donate money towards the end of preaching the gospel? No. There was no need for that. He had done that before without much to show for it. True, it was the financial success of Pastor Wollia his schoolmate and friend that attracted him to the gospel business in the first and last place. Within only three years of Pastor Wollia establishing his own Christ's ministry called Christ Redemption Church, he erected a sprawling bungalow in his home village and three in different parts of Sirama, which he was renting out to tenants and collecting mind-boggling rents. He also had many automobiles on the road and personally drove a Lexus jeep. His two daughters were both in the United Kingdom in the best universities in the world. It was Gojang's reasoning that if a man could have all these and still be entitled to heaven, if there was such a place, then being a minister of God was the sweetest position one could get himself into. He set about getting into it by obtaining a bank loan to acquire a building for his church and put into place the necessary things of luxury that would attract a large followership, make them comfortable, and with a soothing balm, coax them into donating for the work of God. Though things had not been moving at the jet pace he thought they would, he had somehow been able to break even by repaying the loan he obtained from the bank. But breaking even was far from his ships coming home, and he was desperate to see them home sooner than later. What was the use having one's ships at sea all the days of one's useful life only to receive them in the evening when he was shaping up for the grave or even to arrive with him already there?

His source of consolation was that he knew he had what it takes to succeed in the church ministry. He was intelligent; he could preach with tongues of fire, he could persuade; What could he not do? But this source of consolation also always turned out to be his source of dismay. If he could preach like Pastor Wollia, why wasn't he as successful? He knew it took Wollia only three years in the ministry business to acquire all he knew him to have. Why couldn't he at least come near to having half of what Wollia had in three years now that he was six years old in the business? What was more, if he didn't have Wollia's Midas touch, he had tried to benefit from his winning ways by inviting him to his church to preach so that he would not only reap a windfall, but see where he was lacking and make amends. On each occasion, he had personally been in church to watch and hear Wollia preach, not only to benefit therefrom, but to ensure Wollia did not get to some dirty tricks or mischief while preaching in the church. On such occasions, there was nothing in the words and action of Wollia he could hold suspect. His words and countenance were those of a minister of God calling on his children to donate generously towards the propagation of his words in the Bible. On one of such occasions, Wollia went further to stress why the call for donations was becoming strident in the church. He said it was because the second coming of Jesus Christ which would end the toil and persecution his followers were being subjected to by the evil world has been hinged by Jesus Christ himself on when his words have reached the whole humanity. Since Jesus has obviously put a condition to be fulfilled before his second coming to rescue his followers from the wicked system of things in the world, it was for them who were desirous of Christ's second coming to fulfill this condition to be entitled to his second coming and their salvation predicated on it. 'Hear what the Holy Bible says!' Wollia cried:

> And as he sat
> upon the Mount
> of Olives, the
> disciples came
> unto him
> privately saying,

tell us when shall these things be, and what shall be the sign of your coming and of the end of the world?

And Jesus answered and said unto them, take heed that no man deceives you. For many shall come in my name saying, I am the Christ and shall deceive many.

And you shall hear of wars and rumors of war. See that ye are not troubled: For all these things shall come to pass, but the end is not yet.

For nation shall rise against nation; and kingdom against kingdom; and there shall be famine and pestilence and earthquakes in divers places. All these are the beginning of sorrows.

Then shall they deliver you up to be afflicted and shall kill you; and ye shall be hated of all nations for my namesake. And many false prophets shall arise and shall deceive many. And because iniquity shall abound, the love of many shall wax cold.

And this gospel of the kingdom shall be preached in all the world for a witness unto all the

world and then
the end shall
come.

'Mark the last verse my brethren!' he cried, beaming at Pastor Gojang's flock. 'Christ will not come to save us from the evil system of things enumerated in the verses we have just read unless and until his word has been preached to all the inhabitants of the earth as a witness to them so that nobody on the day of judgment shall raise not hearing the gospel as a defense against divine punishment. What then are we expected as beneficiaries of his second coming to do to hasten that coming?' he asked and paused. When it appeared his question had found a hold in the hearts of the majority of the flock, he resumed, 'preach the word my brethren. That's what we are expected to do to hasten Christ's second coming. But, obviously, not all of us can preach as our calling and talents are not the same. To some, the Lord has given the talent of acquiring money and to others the talent to preach the gospel. But since we must all be seen to be preaching the gospel, those who make the money should make it available to those in the field preaching the gospel and this form of preaching is perfectly and wholesomely approved by the lord of host.'

'The smart, canting crook! The son of a gun!' Pastor Gojang exclaimed as he sat thinking over Wollia's interpretation of the Sermon on the

Mount on the aspect of Jesus Christ putting a condition to his second coming and the necessary connection between fulfilling that condition with donating money to the church. 'The smart, canting crook!' he exclaimed again. No wonder Wollia has been shoveling in the money while he has been raking it in. This must be his winning formula, he thought, excitedly. 'But it can't be,' he murmured, sadly on a second thought. After all what was collected that Sunday as church offering fell far short of his expectations and in fact what was collected in Wollia's first sermon in his church. His mind immediately suspected sabotage and betrayal. 'Could it be that Wollia introduced this new dimension in his preaching to scare potential donors from doing so if they felt Christ's second coming was not something they were excited about? That must be it,' he thought gloomily. How many of his flock looked forward to the second coming of Christ with hope and happiness as beneficiaries thereof. Come to think of it, did he himself and even Wollia with all his affected piety, look forward to Christ's second coming with feelings of impatience and great expectation? Speaking for himself, he knew his mind suffered no such agitation. The agitation of his mind was how to come by means to live a comfortable life here and now. The hereafter and a Christ second coming were skewed matters his mind was happier without. As for Wollia, he knew him as a mere Holy Willie who would be a million times happier with his loot without the threat of Christ's second coming. He would definitely not give a fig to accelerate that coming. 'The smart betraying devil!' Gojang cried in agony. 'Let me tell you, I am not going to take this lying low. I am coming for you and when I get you where I want, I will give it to you.' Anxious emotions swarmed over him leaving him lame.

Chapter Eight

Even before the Prince hit the high street, he had made up his mind not only to leave Famla his hometown, but the Democratic Republic of Expero altogether. He knew not only his parents would be looking for him, but the law as well. But how would he leave Expero as cash-strapped as he was and without an international passport and a visa?

The Prince was not brilliant for nothing. Neither was he a member of the Hell-benders for nothing. He soon resolved to go into hiding, stage one or two robberies, get enough money to feed and transport himself by road to Expero's nearest border town where he would slip into Dameta undetected. Once inside Dameta, he was sure he would get lost and be as anonymous in the Dametan assorted crowd as a grain of sand from the road would be when dropped into the sand of an ocean beach. However, in all these, what counted against him more than anything else was the great distance between Famla and Expero's border towns. But even this did not shake his resolve to leave Expero for Dameta.

With his fear of the law and his resolve to leave Expero, when he hit the highway, he found himself dropping off it again to trek under the cover of the forest until he hit a shanty town to provide him with his next meal and with luck, his ticket to slip out of Expero. As he walked in the woods of Famla, his mind kept contracting and elongating in fear and remorse – things he had never felt before. Suddenly his younger brother whom he knew he had killed on account of a radio became dear to him. How could he have done such a thing? he cried. At a point, he was so gripped by fear and remorse that he experienced a shamming death. He could not move. How could he have killed Sil? He looked at the small radio in his hand and flung it away with a curse. 'Oh God! how could I have killed Sil my brother?' he wept, squatting by a shrub like the priest of Manasa the goddess of the snake cult in Bengal. Even as young as he was, he suspected diabolism to have pushed him to the act of killing Sil. But who could be interested in him to practice diabolism on him? He sat down, his hands covering his face, and cried himself weak.

Whether it was his weeping that attracted the snake or it only happened by was not clear to the Prince. As he raised his head from his palms, he saw a snake metres away from him raising its own head. Instinctively, he reached for his fighting knife inside his hip pocket but otherwise remained motionless looking straight at the snake. As he pulled the knife, the snake slithered towards him. He threw himself flat on his face while swinging the knife in his hand upward. The knife caught the snake on its abdomen and divided it into two. The Prince stood up, sweat pouring from his face and fear gnawing at his heart. What a close shave he had just had with death!

From there, he made up his mind not to give in to sorrow the way he had, which had nearly cost him his life. Those who were dead, were dead and no good could be done for them by weeping. It was for him still living to take such measures as would ensure his not joining them, that is, if he still cared for life; and he did. He went and retrieved the radio where he had flung it and moved on. It made no difference if he left it there, he told himself. The harm had already been done. He would not end up like Judas Iscariot betraying Jesus and losing the betrayal money.

Sometime after dusk, he came to Timani a small fishing village near a big lake. It was like many small villages and towns in Expero yet to enjoy the wonders of electricity. The President of Expero had said electricity as its name implies, was meant only for cities, not small towns and villages. They should wait until some egghead comes up with electritown or electrivillage. For now, it was electricity that was available and his government was busy giving it to the cities.

The Prince arrived Timani to find almost the entire male population out at the lake fishing. Fishing in Timani was mainly done in the night. It was to be expected that Timani, being not too far from Famla, the Prince would have heard of it if he had not been there. He had done both, and as a matter of fact, knew the village very well. Knowing what he knew about it, he made for the house of Timani fishermen union leader with whom he had heard the fishermen sometimes kept their union money.

When he arrived the house, he crouched behind a room and listened intensely for any male voice in the house, but heard none. What he could hear were two distant female voices, an indication the men were out at the lake. From the sound of the women voices, he could also detect they were not in a room near him. He walked round the house and found them sitting outside the house warming themselves by an evening fire.

This was his opportunity and he must take it by the forelock. Quickly he slipped into a room through a back window that was open. Being of little stature, he experienced little difficulty doing so. It was a woman's room.

With pessimism, he conducted a quick search using a lantern inside the room, but found nothing. The same way he entered, he got out of the room and entered the next one, which again turned out to be that of a woman. Panic began to grip him. He was conscious of losing time. All the same, he conducted a search, and to his surprise, found a bundle of dirty kusrah notes tucked under a mattress. His weariness left him. 'Money, oh dear money,' he whispered to himself. 'Money, oh dear, heavenly money.' He quickly tucked the money into his pocket and rushed to the window. In his haste, he did not notice a small tin he took care not to land on when he entered the room. He kicked it with his left leg. The sound it made could have woken the dead and the woman in whose room he had removed the money came rushing in, her mind on the money her husband gave her to keep for him. But before she could enter the room, the Prince had smashed the lantern throwing the room into darkness. That should have warned her not to go in. But overwhelmed by the dire consequences of losing the money, she did not pause to take thought on her safety as she plunged into the dark room and into the Prince's waiting knife. With considerable violence, he drove the knife into her guts, pulled it out with the same violence and drove it into the stomach of the second woman who also came blundering into the room following the screams of her mate. The Prince was not done yet. He reached for two little children crying around the fire outside the house; tied them together with a rope and hurled them into the fire to roast with the fish roasting there, then swept out of the house.

The house owner and the leader of Timani fishermen association arrived the house to find it reduced to a slaughterhouse. Lamentation and pandemonium broke loose.

The Prince was full of excitement when he hit the forest once more as a bushranger with no limits to his capabilities. But as he marched on, he could hear one or two butterflies fluttering in his stomach, a sure indication hunger was closing in on him. His weariness returned with a vengeance.

Why didn't I remove the fish roasting in that damn house? he thought despairingly. An angry bug gnawed at his heart with an insane rapidity. He stopped walking to consider going back to get the fish, but considered the risk too high. He was in a dilemma. If he did not go back and did not meet another village nearby to prey on, he would be in serious trouble with his stomach ulcer. Already, he could feel his stomach burning like an eyeball on pepper. He was sure if he did not get food very soon, the money he was holding would be of no use to him. Gradually, he started retracing his steps back to Timani, all his ears flagged up for a warning sound or noise. He did not move far when his keen ears picked the barking of dogs and faint noises of people. He stopped walking and listened. Then he heard lamentations, swearing of oaths and angry curses. Still, he did not move. He wanted to be sure they were not baying at the moon. As he stood listening, the barking of dogs and the shouting of people grew louder and nearer. He knew then they were not baying at the moon but at him. He started running in circles and howling like wolves. The villagers on hearing the howling of wolves were scared stiff and started calling on their dogs to retreat, and they did as the wolves howled louder.

Feeling reasonably safe after the villagers and their dogs withdrew their pursuit, he sat down to rest and consider his most pressing problem – food. How was he to get it in the piscatorial village without compromising his fragile security? Not knowing another nearby village to prey on, he yielded to depression cursing the excitement that deprived him of the fish in the fire. Panic was fast taking over his mind and eating up his confidence. But, after sometime, the wolf in him came alive again. He was once more a bushranger on the wings of the wind moving towards the lake leaving the village by his left. He reasoned that since the villagers had discovered what had happened to one of them – their leader for that matter, they would desert the lake for a moment to commiserate with their grieving companion. If there was any food there, he was sure he would have an uninterrupted feast. He was right on both scores. The lake was like a graveyard when he got there and there was fish roasting by a big fire on the sand. Round the fire laid fresh fish and roasted ones all mixed up. Quickly, he packed the roasted and fresh fish into a big polythene bag lying on the sand near the fire. What could not enter, he cut into pieces, marched on the sand then veered off again.

Chapter Nine

Against his suspicion, pastor Gojang did not find out that pastor Wollia's sermon on the need to hasten Christ's second coming by donating generously to the church was schemed to do him in. On the contrary, his source informed him Wollia had on occasions delivered similar sermons in his own church with resounding success. He was stunned as he was bewildered. What was the trouble with his own church? Could it be a case of the same seed sown on different soils, some yielding and others not? It must be unless there was more to it than meet the eye. Then his eyes opened. Here was it! Wollia must be using diabolical means to coax his flock into donating generously to his church. He could not put it past Wollia to go to any diabolical extent if it would serve his end. Presently, he called to mind his escapade with Wollia to a spiritualist and herbalist home while they were still in school. The spiritualist whose name was Wegang had an awesome reputation for resolving the most complex of problems. So revered was he in metaphysical and occultic medicine that he was reputed to possess clairvoyant powers and ability to influence supernatural forces. His reputation then rang through the Siramian satellite town of Marabi where he lived like the bell of a local railway station. He and Wollia had gone to employ his services to enhance their academic performances in all examinations and to enchant in their favor the hearts of two girls in their class who had caught their fancy.

The decision to see the spiritualist had arisen out of his differences with Wollia on their dismal performance in a particular examination. While he had attributed it to their lack of commitment to studies, Wollia had read lack of supernatural aid to it.

'How do you suppose a crawling mind like Hamis, whose programmed brain revolves around the warped details of classroom lecture notes, would always excel us in examinations when we go beyond lecture notes to the published works of masterminds in the library?' Wollia had asked with a severe bearing that beseemed the issue in council. 'Gojang boy, open your eyes wide. Some guys in this class are onto some dirty tricks and I wouldn't be surprised if it is only you and I who are left holding empty cans before the damn gods of the library. Boy, we are not all on a level playing field,' he said with the wise air of a man of the world.

'What are you saying? Can you be more explicit?' he said with a puzzled expression on his face.

'I didn't know you were such a raw youth in matters of this sort,' Wollia said smirking over an advantage. 'Not to worry. I will tell you what has been happening under your nose without you seeing it.'

Wollia then went on to explain to him in such graphic details as his own smattering knowledge of the issue in handling would allow, how other students including Hamis who had always topped their class in all examinations had been using performance enhancing supernatural means to their chagrin. He alluded to a similar opportunity for themselves which would not only attend to their academic excellence, but would also conduce to their emotional gratification by swaying in their favor the fledgling minds of Henda and Ekoro the two girls in their class who enjoyed the fantasies of their hearts.

The next day found them on the way to Wegang's shrine. Wollia led the way with a rare sense of purpose that attends only missions of destiny. They met Wegang sitting in his shrine like Scylla* opposite Charybdis.* Assorted marks and tattoos adorned the upper part of his body where a shirt should have been. From his right arm hung a horsetail one of the grimoires of his office. There were chalk marks indicating the part of the shrine ordinary humans could tread and the part inhabited only by spirits and he the medium of their manifestation. Without condescending to an introduction of the object of their presence in his shrine, Wegang, like the priest of Delphi,*

A six headed monster who sat over a dangerous rock opposite Charybdis.

In odyssey, a dangerous monster that dwelt under a rock opposite Scylla, and three times a day swallowed and threw up the water of the sea.

A Greek oracle that foretold the future.

proceeded to divine it by observing the various postures of three cowry shells he had artfully thrown on the floor upon their arrival.

'You are on a twin-mission.'

They nodded their heads.

'Your last examination results and two girls of your dreams.'

Wollia nodded, Gojang stammered a surprise.

'For both, I have solutions if only you would cross River Kiryanga with me to the land of the living dead,' Wegang said, his face slightly sagging in response to the grave import of his statement to himself.

River Kiryanga was reputed in Marrabi and other satellite towns of Sirama and even in the capital city itself as the river beyond which a man seeking divine intervention of a cultic character, should direct his steps; because there, ancient men in touch with the supernatural world resided. *Yon, yonder River Kiryanga* was a common phrase on the lips of believers in the awesome powers that lay beyond the river. It brought to mind, benevolent and malevolent supernatural presence beyond the river.

Wegang's proposition for Gojang and Wollia to cross River Kiryanga with him was rightly understood by Wollia in a metaphorical sense of them supplying him with such means as would enable him cross the river and seek on their behalf the favor of the spirits beyond River

Kiryanga. After paying the fees demanded by Wegang, they left with a brown powdery substance, two silver rings to be worn on the index finger of the right hand and with a promise to comply with all the conditions of using the occultic articles to maximum effect. Four months later, they returned to Wegang, like Croesus* the king of Lydia, with a cheerless story of failure. His charms had simply not worked. Their performances in the last examination were worse than those that first brought them to him. As for the hearts of the girls which Wegang had said would leap towards them and never return upon pronouncing their names to the four winds of the earth on a road junction early in the morning, their hearts did leap, but not towards them, but away from them. They had observed with dismay the girls who before their visit to Wegang were merely indifferent to them, suddenly becoming hostile towards them after their adventure. Wegang attributed the failure of the charms to another failure – their failure to comply with all his conditions. Though he knew he did not buy the expensive perfume that Wegang said they should buy for the rituals that would give them the results they wanted, Gojang in his mind doubted the powers of Wegang.

____

* *King of Lydia in whose favor, the priest of Delphi prophesied that if he crosses Halys, he will destroy a mighty empire. It turned out that the mighty empire destroyed was his own. He met defeat at the hand of Cyrus the Persian King when he crossed the Halys to invade Cappadocia.*

After the fiasco that was the Wegang affair, Gojang observed Wollia experimenting with several occultic persuasions long after he had given up on the fantasies of such persuasions. With these antecedents riveting in the imagination fertile mind of Gojang, he could clearly see Wollia's ardent pursuit of diabolical means paying off in his manipulation of his flock. He could visualize Wollia's importunacy wearing down by exerting installments the obstinacy of supernatural powers in the same manner the importunacy of the allegorical woman Christ spoke about wore down to submission the obstinate judge who neither feared God nor regarded man. *

'Damn me! Why didn't I see the matter in this light before?' he lashed at his apparent stupidity. 'To think I have been looking out for Wollia's Midas touch through the door when all the while he has been on the window behind me laughing at me.' His mouth foamed from the sheer irritability of it all.

---

* A widow who persistently a judge who neither feared God nor regarded man for justice against someone who had harmed her. her persistence wore down the judge and he attended to her demand for justice, less she wears him down completely by her persistent request: Luke 18:1-5.

Chapter Ten

When Josira fled their dingy home on the day of her final disillusion with her amorous affiliation to her father, she ran into the grubby home of Kargan to live with him. But for the filial relationship between her and Mimono, an interested observer of her flight might view it as she falling into the hand of Scylla while trying to avoid Charybdis. Kargan giving her a lot of money when she was living with her father, she thought there was more where what he was giving her was coming from and wanted to be at the fountain of *the healing water of river Jordan.* Unknown to her, however Kargan sparing Mimono's abuse of paternity, was by all account a worse financial alternative to Mimono. As an economic index, Kargan viewed life in the pottage terms of Esau.* Pawn whatever you might, so long as that would fetch you a meal. Worse, unlike his prototype, Kargan did not see dignity in any form of labor beyond stealing from others. He suspected in the labour of others culpable folly and it was his office to ridicule such folly by stealing from them whenever he happened upon the opportunity. He nursed a majestic contempt for all entrepreneurs of industry whose direction of effort tended in an opposite direction to the official bias of his mind.

** An Israelite who sold his birth right as first son to his junior brother Jacob for a pot of red stew: Genesis 25:27-34.*

He perceived the whole business of life as a rare opportunity for him to grace the somber earth with his graceful dancing steps and dazzle the languorous skies with his scintillating songs. When hunger stepped in to remind him of the need for work, he went to steal from idiots who had time to work, and he stole only for his stomach. Whoever was hungry should go and have a cut where he did. With his stomach full, he went to drink and came back late at night announcing his presence in the neighborhood in songs and dances. At home, he would find Josira weeping in hunger and anger. He would ask if she needed some action. If she said food, he would point across to a small filling station telling her to go and get money there for her meal and probably his. If she did not move, he would pounce on her, beat her black and blue, tear off her clothes and commence a different assault on her. In so many ways, it could be said Kargan turned out to be everything Mimono on the verge of death suspected and said he was. Also, as it turned out, Mimono's death rattles on how Kargan would meet his end were as prophetic as any prophecy could be. Josira did to Kargan what Kargan caused Mimono to do to himself.

To return to Josira's cohabitation with kargan, Josira played it cool on the surface behaving like the brainless moron Kargan had always called her. Below the surface, however, she was seething with disappointment that Kargan far from having *the healing waters of river Jordan* was in fact a drought and a desert. Her plans of vengeance were well thought out and rehearsed for effect. For one, she did not cross the street to the filling station as Kargan used to tell her. Instead, she stole from him. When he had money on him, she stole some of it during his drunken slumber. When he thought something was missing, he could not pin it on her. It could have fallen off as he danced home or it could have been picked. Out of what she pinched from him, she fed herself and put some away. When she thought she had saved a reasonable sum to meet her purpose of desertion, she gave him in full measure a dose of the overkill Mimono gave himself. On the night it happened, Kargan returned home drunk, danced out and spilling obscenities everywhere to find her looking calm and ravishing.

'Now my sweet…,' he blubbered. 'You look delicious,' he paused in his dancing and spluttered further. 'You need some real hot…' he drooled away.

'No, not a real hot…sweet …; I need a sweet …,' she said with all the lewd gesticulations of a tamed prostitute. 'Oh, how I need a sweet…'

Kargan tore away his clothes. She tore away hers. Minutes later, Kargan was snoring in a fitful sleep. She went into action. From under the bed, she brought out the razor-sharp knife she had bought for her vengeance. Soothingly, she turned Kargan who was all in the nude faced up; then neatly severed his entire genitals and dropped them on his face. Pain ripped through Kargan like the tips of a million needles bringing him out of his slumber in earth-quaking screams. By then, she was already slamming the door behind her on the run. But she needed not run as nobody heeded Kargan's screams which whirred for only a moment before he lay still in death.

Chapter Eleven

The Journey of the Prince into Dameta was long, painful and eventful, but he made it without a passport and without a visa. After running for about thirty minutes with the provisions he stole from Timani clutched to his chest, he felt the berth between him and the fishermen of Timani was not one they could cover in one big leap. He sat down to eat and regain his spent energy before trudging on. He had scarcely finished eating one fish when a sudden cloudburst shot down big raindrops splattering through the forest. A long lightning that seemed to split the sky into two revealed a mahogany tree standing not too far from an oak tree. Gathering the polythene bag with the fish, he dashed towards the mahogany tree, but on a second reflection the oak tree offered a better fortress against the pelting raindrops, he alternated towards it. He silhouetted himself against the tree trunk like a hunted reptile. A second lightning longer than the first, flashed across the stormy sky followed by a deafening blast of thunder that threw the Prince down on his back. When he got up, the mahogany tree adjacent the oak tree he was sheltering under was a blasted stump. To think he had actually wanted to take cover under that tree. He shuddered like a child unable to say boo to a goose. Could invisible means be at work against him? First, there was the snake, and now this thunder. Could the ghost of Sil, like the ghost of

Duncan, be after him so soon? For a moment, he was mystified by the inexplicable.

The rainstorm whistling past him sounded like an elegy to his bewildered sensibilities. When he was able to govern his emotions better, he went in search of a less unnerving place to pass the night.

Without an international passport, a visa and sufficient funds, he decided, in the course of the night, to board a bus in the morning from the nearby town of Gustan to the border town of Ogatah. From Ogatah, he would burrow his way out of Expero to Dameta through the mangrove forest.

His journey through the mangrove forest, which he had feared would be a nightmare or even end in an aborting fiasco by the tongue of a snake, turned out to be a free sail.

He stayed in Yakon a Dametan border town for three days before travelling to Sirama the capital of Dameta. He arrived Sirama in the evening with only one hundred kusrah in his pocket. While walking listlessly along Redshell, a backstreet of Sirama, he came by a roadside restaurant and bar bustling with people, drinks and food. The butterflies of hunger fluttered in his stomach. The one hundred kusrah in his pocket was not money in Dameta and so he could not use it to buy food. Still, he moved towards the restaurant against the protest of his empty pockets.

There were about two or three empty seats around two tables. He chose one and sat down, careful not to step on any of the empty bottles strewn all over the floor. Around the table he sat were two men drinking beer and talking boisterously though they were supposed to be having a conversation. They were completely oblivious of the Prince's arrival on the scene. While one of them was a beanpole with a somewhat fell countenance and a lantern jaw, the other was squatty coming in height perhaps to the beanpole's abdomen.

'Yes, boy, what do we do for you?' a funny-looking waiter asked, hovering over the Prince, his eyes frisking him for money, finding none, became stiff and stern.

'What you have done to the others,' the Prince said in an even voice.

'By which you mean …food?'

'Yes.'

'Are you sure you have the money to pay for it? I don't like trouble.'

'Money is a dumb companion and an unseen customer,' the Prince said, off key. 'And as for you not liking trouble, I regret to say even your birth was not without some trouble to somebody, and I suppose you won't wonder who that somebody was.'

At this point, the squatty man sitting nearer the Prince stopped talking and gave the Prince a curious and thoughtful look as the latter continued.

'You see why trouble is inevitable in this miserable life? Your father had to bang your mother and your mother had to scatter her legs for you to fall out; plenty trouble for them both you will agree. So, what right have you my friend to hate trouble?'

At this, the restaurant burst into laughter.

The waiter doubly provoked, slapped the Prince on his cheek and hauled him up. 'Idiot, you don't splutter that kind of gibberish on me!' Again, he slapped the Prince; this time across the face. The squatty man sitting next to the Prince's empty seat jumped up kicking an empty bottle on the floor and shot himself between the Prince and the waiter. In a cold, colourless voice, he told the waiter to steer clear of the Prince and he did without an argument. There was something about the squatty man that made the waiter's skin to creep. It was as frightening as it was uncanny. This sneaky aspect of the squatty man was not lost on the Prince as he came on again more confidently than before, 'food man!'

'Filthy country boy,' the waiter said with a swank, 'no food for you without seeing the colour of your money first.'

'Please, give him food,' the squatty man came in again for the Prince in that same cold, colourless voice of his. Again, that thing about him sent the waiter to the kitchen to bring the food. After placing the food before the Prince, he asked, 'who will pay, should you fall short?'

'The devil will pay,' the squatty man said, this time in a voice full of menace and predation. 'Scram!' The waiter slopped away with such awe that he could not show up to collect the money but the head-chef.

As the Prince ate, he kept throwing admiring glances at the squatty man wondering who the devil he was. Whoever he was, he seemed to vest in the Prince a wild confidence that reeked violence. The squatty man on his part for once never looked in the prince's direction while he ate. He was once more hooked to his boisterous conversation with the beanpole who though, the exact opposite of the squatty man in physique, was his replica in words and manners. The Prince having eaten to his satisfaction, relaxed back on his seat completely at ease while he waited for the beginning of trouble.

Some minutes later, the head chef, fat and flabby waddled to the Prince's table and flung his bill at him, then stretched out his hand to collect the money.

The Prince looked at the extended hand unimpressed and said, 'sorry man. I ain't gotta buck on me. Whacha gona do?'

Again, the squatty man and the beanpole had stopped talking to stare at the oddity called the Prince.

'You have no money?'

'Yes, I have no money.'

'That's interesting, isn't it?' the head chef said, actually not addressing the Prince, but the whole people in the restaurant. 'Here is a louse from hell who has fed fat on my food only to tell me he has no money to pay for what he had eaten; isn't that interesting?'

Some people laughed while others looked curiously at the Prince. By this time, it was getting dark outside.

'Young man, I hope you will appreciate this is not a Father Christmas' restaurant. Stop kidding and dig out some money to pay for what you have eaten. You can't just walk in here, tuck food to the brim of your throat and walk out without your pocket coughing out a dime. It just isn't done. Even in a Father Christmas' shop, you don't enter without parting with some chips to the gateman. Come on, stop kidding and let me go about frying my other fishes,' Again, he extended his hand to the Prince

'Fat oaf, I told you I ain't gotta fig; but since you pester me, what I get I give you,' the Prince said, drew out his fighting knife and lounged at the chef who in the least expectation of violence could only stagger to one side as the Prince came flying at him. Before he could recover his balance, the Prince who had narrowly missed him had landed and was lounging at him again. This time, the knife caught him squarely in his heart. Jerking the knife savagely out of the falling body of the chef, the Prince wheeled round to face everybody with the knife reeking blood and his small body vibrating with action. All these things happened only in the spate of three seconds. By the time the dead body of the chef thudded on the floor, pandemonium, was reigning in the restaurant with a fell cacophony. A tall, huge man rushed at the prince from behind a counter, but was stopped midway by the Prince's knife that came flying from a smart throw by the Prince. He took it fully in his belly, coughed blood, before thudding home. The squatty man with a pistol in hand, took hold of the Prince and ran out with him together with the beanpole into a parked BMW and drove away into the dark night like birds from hell.

Taldon, for that was the squatty man's name, turned out to be the leader of an armed robbery gang known as *Megabug Jailers* with their den in Pamsi. The beanpole, called Recodo, was also a member of the *Megabug Jailers* from which Sirama had taken a heavy bashing.

The *Megabug Jailers*, though parading tough characters, engaged mainly in gold snatching. According to this established practice, they referred to themselves as goldbugs. Their obsession with the yellow metal sprang from the commonplace economic sentiment of the value of gold and its portability.

Apart from being the leader of the Megabug Jailers, Taldon was also a member of the snake cult of Sirama – a bizarre secret society. The snake cult denounced God, crawling around the snake as an object of worship. Impressed to the marrow by the Prince's rare disposition and mental projections, Taldon committed himself to rearing him into a deadly and ferocious robber of gold.

Housed, fed and clothed by Taldon, the prince proved a worthy apprentice with a flourishing ambition that often outstripped Taldon's narrow inclinations. It was always a remark on Taldon's lips that the Prince was bound for the roof, by which he meant the Prince was destined for greatness. Paying regard to this estimation of the Prince, he initiated him into the snake cult, which was an armed robbers' academy of sort.

The snake cult of Sirama had its shrine in the northern outskirts of the city. It was a round building of stones buried fifteen feet below the earth surface. What passed for its door was a round opening with the door also made of stones. The door only opened before and after *waxing the head of the Grand Master* – the cult's euphemism for snake worship. Inside the shrine, there was no single seat or even a folded podium of the floor where the priest of the cult might sit. The only material gracing the shrine was a green carpet that padded the entire floor and walls of the shrine. The only elevation in the shrine was a twenty-centimetre-tall wooden beam with a plateau top standing in the centre of the shrine. Around its trunk twirled a snake with its head lying on the plateau top.

The cult held its meetings once every fortnight between the hours of 3 and 4am. Worship was conducted in a curtain of darkness with only a flickering candlelight casting grotesque shadows on the carpet beneath. Save for tight boxers, worship was in *puris naturalibus** in solidarity with the snake – the Grand Master. The worshippers lay flat on their stomachs forming a circle. Heads flowed out of the inner circle while legs flowed in. Inside the inner circle stood the beam. The cult's priest called the serpenthead would, like every member be on his stomach as he led the worship. However, unlike other members, his head flowed inward towards the beam and the snake. When worship was about starting, the priest gradually rose up snake-like, then fell back to the floor when he had risen full length. His fall would be greeted with chanting of, 'rise the serpenthead, rise! rise the serpenthead, rise!' by all members. At this, the priest would start rising in a queer rhythmic fashion. As he would be rising, the snake coiled on the plateau would uncoil and start rising in tune with the chanting and rising of the priest or rather, the priest in tune with the rising of the snake. When the priest and the snake had risen half way to full height, the priest would fall back on the floor again leaving the snake standing on the plateau. The proper worship would then commence led by the priest in a singsong:

Grand master the canal of knowledge
Grand master the fountain of wisdom
Knowledge the giver of wealth
Knowledge the giver of power
Wisdom the giver of greatness
Please let your canal of knowledge
Please let your fountain of wisdom
Be among your children.

As this sing-song worship went on, the snake would swirl its head about spewing venom on the heads of its worshippers. The singsong ended and the snake resuming its coiled position around the beam, the priest would move on to an exposition of why the snake and the snake alone deserved their worship. Whatever he said, the rest of the members would finish off for him in this order:

When knowledge and wisdom lay hidden in heaven above...
You lay it bare here on earth.
There was a God that was bitter with what you did....
And called you evil.
A God that only felt secured and happy
In the ignorance of his creatures...
What a scandalous God!
A God that pranced in happiness seeing us blind...

What a sadistic God!
In contempt and spite for that God...
We rank you virtuous G-ra-n-d ma-s-ter...

They would shout together in sharp, stabbing voices that would gradually fall into a disturbing silence. Then, abruptly, everybody would jump up from his prostrated position and start prancing about in an unwieldy, unearthly way; singing without any rhythmic pattern:

Pour us the knowledge,
Pour us, pour us, pour us the knowledge, pour us
Pour us the wisdom, pour us,
Pour us, pour us, pour us the wisdom, pour us
Give us the power,
Give us, give us, give us the power, give us.

The snake again would be up on its tail spewing venom on all. The worship over, every cultist would put on his clothes and vanished leaving the priest with the snake inside the shrine. The priest did not leave until dawn.

The Prince pursuing a self-appointed destiny of a distinguished career in gangsterism approved the Megabug Jailers' project of stealing only gold. Such an attitude to him was a celebration of specialization in robbery. Ease of handling and invaluable quality of gold as the underpinning consideration for the Megabug Jailers' choice of gold also met with his approval. High value and portability, the Prince however reasoned gold enjoyed with its sister ornaments – silver and diamond. On this score, he could not understand the preference given by the Megabug Jailers to gold over the other two ornaments. He also could not understand their abstention from money robbery.

Given the wholesale and flourishing terms the Prince conceived his own gangsterism, he came to view Taldon's Megabug Jailers' theft of gold as a little smear on the wall of gangsterism. It was the sort of thing any wire could do and he considered himself above the low devices of any wire.

Chapter Twelve

Sirama the capital city of Dameta was one of the capital cities in Africa that became capital cities by the design of the postcolonial governments. Before the Dametan national government finally decided on Sirama as the capital city, many other towns were touted as possible capitals of the country. In the end, many favorable factors conduced to settle the prevarication in favor of Sirama. Among these factors were the almost virgin state of Sirama, which made for unhindered development, the centrality of the town and its beautiful landscape dotted with imposing hills and mountains. Within a few years of the capital of Dameta moving from Balas to Sirama, Sirama acquired a metropolitan aspect that could aspire for a place in a contest of capital cities. The flock of job-seekers and fortune-hunters in Dameta poured into Sirama by the fall of each day like honey-ants to honey-dew. Being a resident of Sirama became synonymous with being a person of financial clout. Those who by choice of residence or some other circumstances could not live in Sirama were, on occasions of social intercourse with people living in the capital city often embarrassed by the haughty airs of the latter.

Right from the age she became conscious of environment, it has been Josira's burning desire to live in Sirama. When she came to live with Kargan, this desire took a feral complexion. As

Kargan moved from one state of moral derangement to another, her obsession with Sirama raged like a hurricane. When she tipped Kargan over the precipice of limbo, she ascended to the conspicuousness of Sirama.

She arrived Sirama with only enough money to rent a cheap hotel for two nights and perhaps buy a couple of snacks. After that, she would be without a farthing. She found such a hotel in Kuwate a suburb of the city. On bed, her eyes roved over the ceiling of her room while her mind darted to all possible alleys that would lead her out of the financial woods she was in. Lacking training in any proper profession, prostitution that old profession that tends naturally to women at odds with any seemly vocation as farming tends naturally to unlettered men, brazenly recommended itself to her like the messiah of Galilee.* Along this street, she found comfort smiling at her. However, her easy virtue had always shrank from the calling of full-time prostitution, preferring concubinage instead. Marriage as a proposition on the other hand was out of court with her. She would not make any money from marriage. But as a mistress, she would swim in *the healing waters of river Jordan – the healing waters of river Jordan* of the man who becomes the priest of her shrines. She was in no

----

Judas of Galilee who claimed to be messiah only for his followers to disappear after his death: Acts 5:37.

mind to embrace marriage – the gloom of her poor mother, Mekelin.

The following evening, she was out on the streets keen on the proposition of the previous night. Flaunting a beautiful face and a graceful body, debauched faces stuck out of moving vehicles to behold the beauty on parade. Three fanciful cars stopped simultaneously, each leering face from the cars intent on a catch. She chose the most expensive of the lot and hopped in. With this kind of car, *the water of river Jordan* must flow in the channels of the owner of the car.

The man in the car was cold in attitude, savage in countenance and far from handsome in looks. The cold, meaningless smile that hung on his lips without actually touching them gave him the appearance of a smiling wolf. She reached for the car's opening latch. But before her fingers could close on it, the car was already travelling at sixty kilometres per hour, placing her between the choice of a certain death on the road and a probable one in the claws of a wolf. She chose the latter to find the wolf changing into a genial, affable man with a somewhat boyish smile. For all his affected amiability, she told herself to watch out for the wolf while hanging on the boy. All the same, the change in the man did a lot to put her in a relaxed mood, and what he said did more.

'I like scaring people first,' was how he proceeded to explain his uncouth manners. 'When you scare them one moment only to relax them the next moment, the thrills of the happiness are amplified by the preceding fear. For you to enjoy good health, you have to be sick first, you know. By the way, I am Falang; who are you?' he asked with an infectious cheerfulness that completely swept Josira off her guard though she still smiled timidly at him as she said, 'I am Heslin.' This was the name she had adopted for herself after leaving Kargan. This name, she intended to use in Sirama where she intended to spend the rest of her life. It was her way of breaking off with a nasty past.

'Baby, just coming into town?' Falang asked

'Don't I look like a Siramian?'

'I haven't said so; after all, Siramians come in different shapes and sizes. It is the conglomerate of Dametans which the best and the base can lay claim to with high degree of credibility. My baby, you pass for a Siramian.'

'Why then did you ask?'

'Because I haven't seen you in Sirama before.'

'Which is to say you know everybody in Sirama?'

'The pretty ones, yes; the ugly, no! I make it my business to know the beautiful ones, and I think I know them all.'

She laughed. 'You are funny.'

'Any idea where you are heading?' he asked after a brief interlude of silence.

She was jolted to the present and the irksome.

'Well, not exactly,' she stammered. 'There is this cousin of mine residing in this city whose address I was holding, but had unintentionally lost in transit from home to Sirama.'

'I take it that all people who lose things do so unintentionally?'

'I suppose so myself,' she stammered, smarting under the lashing jest in Falang's voice.

'And where is home, if I may ask?'

'Fekolo,' she gave him her adopted village name. 'Who are you for a change?'

'I am what they call a Sambo from the United States of America if you must know.'

'U.S the wonder country?'

'And so Dameta supposed to be.'

'Well, that is what people say.'

'What do you Dametans say?'

'The same, being people.'

'But how dare you, when you have not only failed Sambos like me, but God that wanted to make Dameta the Garden of Eden. How dare you when you have failed everybody, especially we Africans in Diaspora?'

'Before I know it, you will be saying Dameta was actually the Garden of Eden passed to us the true children of Adam and Eve to plunder.'

'And that is how it is! The way I see it, when Africa rolled her drums in Egypt and the world theatre rose to dance, the drums were passed to Dameta for the beating. Unfortunately, Dameta went to sleep leaving the stage to thieving and corrupt characters. Now Dameta is in shambles. Refugees here, refugees there; in a land of milk and honey! Talk of Adam and Eve!' he said with a heavy dose of sarcasm. 'How do you hope to be respected and treated with dignity by other nations when with your own hands, you have ruined your own nation. As if that is not enough provocation, after doing your country in, you run to other countries as political or economic refugees to reap where you have not sown. Let the man who generates a typhoon in his domain with the vain hope of migrating to monsoon climes for a bumper harvest know he will not be a lonely fugitive in his flight. The sand-dust from his ancestral activity is a speedier fugitive that will bear his iniquities to the four winds and the nine suns of the earth aborting the hope of his naivety. Who are the guys to do the fixing while you do the dislocation? Ahh... Assuming they exist,' he said, rhetorically, 'has a sailor any more right to complain of Davy Jones than an idler of idle worms? What right has a pansy to complain of goo? The cowed deserves a slave-fork as surely as the libber his liberty cap. You make your bed, you lie on it. I mean you guys got it all wrong and must go back to the drawing board,' he concluded scarcely aware of her presence in the car.

'You are beginning to sound like a politician to me,' she said, taking a closer look at him. 'I don't want to get mixed up in politics.'

'Cut the politics stuff out of it,' he said with such verbal violence that she had never heard in her life.

'But Falang, why the anger? I am not the President of Dameta. Can't you see I am just an innocent fly in the spider's web?'

'That's where you guys get it all wrong again. There's no innocent fly that gave the requisite struggle and remained in the cobweb. Power is sweet, and in its sweetness lays its potentials of abuse. Any leader will govern arbitrarily if he is sure of a passive followership. You have such followership and so your leaders gravitate to self-seeking ends. What is more, in any society shit turns up in the kitchen and eggs in the toilet, the affairs of men get messy. For the time will never come when shit will roll out an omelette. While other societies place their race-horses on the racetrack, you field tumblebugs leaving your race-horses to suffer the tragedy of unsung geniuses,'

Josira not interested in the subject Falang was obsessed with, said nothing.

Fallang sensing her lack of interest offered her accommodation until she could dig up her cousin. She gladly accepted the offer. That settled, he engaged gears and within minutes they found themselves at his residence on Civil Avenue.

Falang's residence turned out to be a splendid instance of luxury. Whatever ought to be in place for comfort and class was in place.

Whatever was missing was of no consequence in the world of luxury. To start with, the interior walls were covered with wall carpets. On the floor, about three different types of Persian rugs lay on each other. Aquariums of different sizes took occupation of strategic spots in the living room. The life-size television in the living room came to life when they entered the house.

She collapsed on a sofa thrown by her first encounter with the wonders of money. As she stared vacantly at the walls of the house, her numbed mind was yet to settle her warring emotions and fully appreciate where she was. When it did, she accused God of undue favouritism that tended too much to the comfort of the likes of Falang and the misery of her likes. Her resentment was further exacerbated by a song her father used to sing to her:

>Money is not rain that falls on every farm
>It is manna that falls on those
>With a prophecy for a promised land
>Even for them
>There are red seas and deserts to cross
>Money is an oasis
>Many desert birds cannot reach.

Falang who had gone into one of the bedrooms came back into the living room. He was in pyjamas and was carrying a pack of fruit juice and two drinking glasses. He placed the pack of juice and glasses on a stool by the sofa and sat down on the sofa. His boyish manners were on and about him. After patting Josira playfully on her shoulder, he poured the juice into one of the drinking glasses and handed it to her.

Smiling, she received the drink.

'How are you feeling in the house of Jupiter?' he asked.

'Not as bad as you picked me,' she replied, and added, 'thanks to your soothing paradise.'

'You are welcome to the home of Jupiter the god of hospitality.'

'Is this how all houses in Sirama look?'

'Some, yes, some, no.'

'You don't have a wife and children?'

'If I had, we won't be here, will we?'

'I guess not.'

'Fine, baby, that's the way it is. Feel at home and name what you will eat and you will have it.'

'I am not fussy about what goes into my belly; anything will do.'

'That will not do in the house of Jupiter, especially when it has the singular privilege of hosting Lady Diana. You are the best, and only the best will do for you.' He strolled into the kitchen and went about some task. Soon he was back with a slap-up dish Josira had not heard the name.

'It appears your taste in all things is great,' was how she proceeded to tell him what she thought of the food they were eating.

'But I thought in Dameta it is a mark of disrespect to the god of fertility to talk while eating?' he yapped.

'All our gods died three years ago if you don't know; and that includes the god of fertility,' she said.

They both laughed.

The meal over, Josira lay back on the sofa revealing gorgeous thighs and Falang advanced with a blue face spitting debauchery.

Chapter Thirteen

Pastor Gojang in a flash of contempt for Wegang on account of his last encounter with him and on account of a strong desire to be on first hand contact with the solemn mediums of the supernatural world beyond River Kiryanga, decided to breach Wollia's protocol of deferring to Wegang by going straight to the world beyond River Kiryanga. As he moved on the solitary path to the world beyond River Kiryanga in the solemn spirit of the enterprise at hand, he suddenly came upon Chiang, the financial secretary of his church who also cut the picture of a publican overwhelmed by the spirit of an accomplished mission beyond the river. He was in fervent prayer concerning the enterprise just ended beyond the river.

The two men bumped into each other without notice, fell apart in fear, laughed in assuring presence and shrank back in suspicion.

'Where are you coming from?' Gojang asked with a melted heart.

'Where are you going?' Chiang asked, mirth all over his face. He was obviously in a better position than Pastor Gojang and he knew it. At most, all he did in church was count offering and occasionally conduct Sunday service. Gojang had the unenviable job of mounting the pulpit to declare Christ against the world of darkness where the devil belongs and resides. Chiang as well as

Gojang know that Gojang was in enemy territory and woe betide him if what befell the mimickers of Jesus and Paul* befalls him.

'Don't you think it bad manners to answer your Pastor's question with a question?' Gojang asked losing expression and voice.

'Not at all,' Chiang said with all the cheer his face could accommodate. 'You see, it is already evening and therefore more concern should be given to a body and soul straying away from home on this blind path towards the awesome river than one hurrying from it towards home. The lost sheep coming back home is in less danger than the one straying into the forest especially at dusk when the wolf, the hyena and the leopard are abroad.'

'Look Chiang, I don't expect rudeness from you, neither will I take it,' was all Gojang could say to Chiang as he brushed past him and moved nearer River Kiryanga and what he saw as his date with destiny. But if that was all his mouth found to say to Chiang, his heart and mind found more. The moment his back was on him, Gojang's mind raced back to snap him up, dissect him and found him unworthy of his position in the church and dismissed him. This was how his mind proceeded to deal with the audacious, corrupt and diabolical financial secretary it found Chiang to be.

Non-Christ believing Jews who attempted casting out an evil spirit from a man in the manner Jesus and his believing disciples and apostles were doing. They were attacked by the evil spirit and had to flee naked: Acts 19:13-16.

For a moment, he was seized by the most fictitious flight of fancy.

'Who is Chiang?' his mind raged.

'He is the financial secretary of your church,' his heart replied.

'I know that, I know that,' his mind raged even more. 'When I asked who is Chiang, I mean what type of man is he?'

'Well, for that, Chiang is the man who touches the church money before you and in fact any other person in the church.'

'I like that, and what again?'

'That pockets some of the money and renders the rest useless by his touch through the use of evil spirits.'

'Yes.'

'His touch on the money of the church renders it worthless and also discourages the congregation from donating to the church.'

'Yes.' By this time, he was no longer moving but standing in one spot, his wits totally deranged and his mind in a white stupor of anger.

'In a sense, Chiang can be said to be the man that is set against your financial success in the process of his commitment to his own financial success. You, as it were, is the donkey that carries his manure home.'

'Terrible, Terrible!' Pastor Gojang cried in agony. 'Chiang, it is all over with you in GCGC, it is all over with you with money; it is all over with you with life. I, Pastor Gojang has spoken,' he mourned, turning to head back home.

At once, it became clear to him why Chiang not on the same street with him in enterprise or ability was nonetheless wealthier than he. Not that he had not had occasions to brood over Chiang's financial success, because he had and even suspected him of stealing some of the church money while counting offering after church service. Though he took to watching him closely whenever he was counting church offering, while pretending not to do so, he had never caught him stealing. This being the only way he could investigate his suspicion against Chiang, he had to take it that Chiang had some other means of making money unknown to him beside his clerical job at the Ministry of Information. Also being not in the same calling, he did not so much envy Chiang's financial success as he did that of Wollia. After all, it was not Chiang that excited him into founding Give Christ the Glory Church, but Wollia. Therefore, his competition was with Wollia and not Chiang. However, with this new revelation by his heart, the position was roundly changed. Chiang from now on should be the man to watch and taken care of. Common sense immediately told him that even if he could preach like angels or Jesus Christ himself and make people not only to bring their widow's mite but to mortgage their body parts as well to get money to bring to the church, that money would not come as

Chiang would discourage it from coming; and the little that does come, he would make worthless. Everything was as clear to him as the open sky. He could clearly see why his heart-melting sermons had failed to stir the hearts of his sheep to give, while the little that was given never yielded any good like the cursed money of Judas Iscariot. On the first count, he found justification for his vaunted ability to preach like Pastor Wollia failing to stir the hearts of his flock into donating their widow's mite. On the second count, he found why even the little that was donated never seemed to get the church anywhere. How could it, when part of it went into Chiang's pocket, and the rest into the wind he turned it. Though his eyes had never caught Chiang stealing, since his heart said so, it must be so. As poor as offerings were in the church, he felt and thought he has always felt they accomplished far too less than they ought to.

'I can kill you for this!' he cried beside himself with grief. 'Believe me, I can kill you for this. Though a scheming devil like you is incapable of holding any belief, still against the current of your unbelief, I want the devil in you to know that I, Pastor Gojang, is capable of murder. Yes, murder for the sake of the church. No wonder the idiot has the insolence to laugh at me as I go about trying to remedy the poor finances of the church. The crude impudence of the bastard! No wonder the devil, like Satan his master, has not the slightest feeling for the church and its people.'

Mentioning people, Gojang's mind veered off in another direction. Which people was he talking about? he wondered. The people of his church? No, they could not be! Hadn't they been the very people that voted Chiang as the financial secretary of the church for three consecutive times against his wish? Immediately his mind suspected conspiracy and sabotage, and his nose smelled a rat – a very rotten rat indeed. Could it be that his flock is privy to Chiang's thievery and diabolism and he was the only one outside holding an empty can and taking their derision? And why not when it was all to their advantage, though to his ruin. He was bewildered beyond words and started shaking with nausea. It was all right and easy dealing with Chiang. But it was suicidal dealing with his entire flock. His mind faltered at the mere thought and returned to the easy prey and with good reason. If Chiang was dealt with, his diabolism would be dealt with, and if his diabolism was dealt with, the flock, if privy to its use, would be free and deterred thereby.

'Then against Chiang, I go,' he said as he ran back home.

Chapter Fourteen

The Prince did not last long with Taldon's Megabug Jailers. He conceived of criminality in more wholesale terms than the retail conception of Taldon and his Megabug Jailers. While Taldon saw armed robbery only as a means of survival, the Prince saw it as a means of survival and attaining political relevance. Pen robbers had used their pens to rise to political eminence as armed soldiers had used their guns to intrude into the political calculus. He, the Prince, would balance the political equation by hybrid means that pertain both. When he decided to leave the Megabug Jailers, he left them according as their rude culture would recommend – without notice, without warning.

Five years after leaving the Megabug Jailers, the Prince banded together six men of similar disposition into the most lethal and decisive armed robbery gang ever to be conceived by men. This was the Cimmerian Brotherhood. While having a loose proposition of armed robbery, the Cimmerian Brotherhood nevertheless concentrated their robbery operations on jewelry shops, banks and bureau-de-change. Each Cimmerian was a specialist of sort. Starting with the Prince, he was the chief investigator, master planner and smart knife-thrower.

Second in order of capability was Makol – conman, chief marksman who could not only shoot fast and accurate, but could also throw knives with more deadly precision than even the Prince. He was a man with immense potentials of outflanking the Prince particularly in the field of action. It was observed that while the Prince was the best brain in scheming robberies, he was wont to be less effective when under the charge of a choking anger that seemed to interfere with his breathing and vision. Then Makol toppled him as the perfect executioner.

Following Makol was Dikask – master key-cutter, masksman and blackmailer. Next to Dikask was Yomoyo the Owl. He earned the owl sobriquet because it was he that specialized in disconnecting electric power to reduce the premises of their robbery into a Cimmerian darkness before the actual robbery. If there was any killing to be done, he did it with chilling and frightening brutality that left nothing even to the imagination of the Prince. When killing, he had no use for a gun or a knife. Nothing tended to his happiness than hearing his victim croak under the squeeze of his murderous hands. After dispatching his victims to the great beyond by such crudities he had trained his bulky hands to wield, he severed their genitals and descended to Cimmeri with them together with his loot. He had forty-five murders to his credit with none pointing in his direction. Whenever Yomoyo was in action, death was always there smiling at his victims.

Then came Jirimi – driver and sentinel. Bringing the rear and by every means the least, was Kokoto who was of little use beyond making up the number and running errands.

The Prince decided which place was to be robbed, went and investigated it, drew up the plan of action then ascended out of Cimmeri with his men, each playing his role with consummate expertise. If long-range killing or conning was required, Makol tasked his skills. If electric power was to be cut, Yomoyo moved in and saw to that. If master keys, blackmailing and masking were called for, Dikask was on hand to meet and break all barriers. But he stopped short of safes where Makol moved in again to throw them open for them to grab and bolt back to Cimmeri unscathed. If there was ever an effective and well-organized set-up, the Cimmerian Brotherhood was one. After over seven years of existence and flourishing as the most fiendish and ruthless underworld organization of armed bandits that ever preyed on humanity, the Dametan police was yet to know there was such a robbery gang as the Brotherhood, least smash it.

The Brotherhood had handled with astonishing success many robbery operations involving highly secured establishments that had gradually led it to believe in its invincibility, though the Prince had always insisted its feeling of invincibility be not suffered to move from confidence to over-confidence. Perhaps, the toughest robbery operation the Brotherhood had tackled before now was that of Oseta bank Suleni. It was an operation the Brotherhood had no choice but kill all the guardsmen and Alsatian dogs on duty; smashed all doors before reaching the vaults which proved trickier than breaking in. Even with an expert hand like Makol, it took them quite a moment of sweating before they could get at any eweka in the safes. And when they eventually did, they could hear the sirens of the police speeding towards the bank. Still, they were able to melt back into Cimmeri without material or human casualties. But it now seemed the case of Oseta bank was a child's play compared to the National Bank scenario the Prince was painting for them. And they knew the Prince to be the last person to exaggerate. If he said robbing the National Bank was going to be a tough assignment, a tough assignment it would be.

'This is the way to proceed,' the Prince said, his voice thin and eerie. 'When dealing with an organization as secured with the latest security apparatus as the National Bank, you don't adopt gun-toting tactics; instead, you try to secure the co-operation of the guys involved. Let's for a moment assume you are able to beat the outer security network and gets close to the safes, how do you open them without the combinations which as I said are with three different people who do not even know each other's combination. Even in the daytime during which we don't operate, we can't burst into the bank pointing our guns at the manager or some other staff to force him to open the safes; because he doesn't have all the combinations. Unless we intend to march him through the streets of Sirama looking for the bank's auditor and I bet none of us would like to do that because it won't take us anywhere. You can begin to see why I said gun-toting tactics simply won't do. But persuasion will do. Anybody can be persuaded given the right approach. Whether tough or lily-livered jacks, all men yield to persuasion depending on the agency of persuasion and the means it employs. The guys involved in the National Bank are tough birds. The manager, a hard-boiled character who goes by the name Smart is the toughest of the lot. A stiff-necked jack – if ever there was one. Before he was cooked, a stone was cooked and the stone was ready first. That's the sort of fellow he is. He was said, while working with a bureau-de-change as treasury manager to have remained unruffled by the threat of a gun-toting youngster who wanted him to submit the keys to the safe to him. He never did and the youngster who couldn't muster enough courage to effect his threat was the worst for it. As he walked out of the bureau-de-change frustrated, he was shot in the back by Smart without the least hesitation.'

'Why not,' a voice rang out of the darkness of Cimmeri as if from a bottomless pit. 'Such should be the nemesis of all idiots that put others before themselves in the name of a dubious pretension called conscience.'

'You can say that again and even more,' the Prince said. 'But this shows you how tough Smart is. The exuberance and wild passion of youth with no firm restrain-guards ought to have scared him, but they didn't.'

'It is surprising,' another voice rang out, 'how a man can become so obsessed with protecting money that is not his? I mean, it screws me silly to think.'

'They certainly don't think that way,' came the Prince again. 'The money certainly is not theirs, but in some cranky way, they tend to believe they are under a charge to defend it.'

'Very well,' another voice came, hostile and burning with excitement of the savage kind. 'I hope they will also deem themselves under a charge to die for it.' The man who spoke these words was a man of action not of thought. Whatever was not well thought before given to him only found consideration in his hands.

'Going by the incidence I have just narrated between Smart the manager and the youngster, it seems they deem themselves under that charge, at least Smart seemed so inclined,' came the Prince again.

'Very well then; we shall again put to test that his inclination,' came another voice cold, flat, menacing. 'If he is Smart, we are *Smash*, and we have never failed to smash a *Smart* we want to smash.'

'Yes,' the Prince interposed. 'But the smashing of the National Bank where *the Lord Mammon* is sitting in this country is going to be a smashing different from the ordinary run of smashing. Money – the Lord Mammon, is sitting on his throne and all the earth worship him. There are no agnostics or atheists, pagans or animists that do not believe or worship the Lord Mammon. There are no Christians, Moslems, Buddhists, Confucians or Shintoists when the Lord Mammon calls for worship. The Lord Mammon is not a jealous God because everyone worships him. We are all gathered in his temple seeking his face, praying for his favor. We all believe in the heaven of his presence and the hell of his absence.'

'True,' enthused Makol. 'The hand of the Lord Mammon is everywhere blessing those he will bless and cursing those he will curse. Omnipresent and omnipotent Mammon heals the sick, gives sight to the blind and legs to the lame. The world is one united bitter family in its thirst for the Lord Mammon. It is one united happy family when the showers of the Lord Mammon drizzle on every one.'

Recovering* money from the National Bank has become one of the most important projects in my life,' continued the Prince. 'So, if I appear

---

* *Recovery was the Prince's euphemism for robbery.*

116

finicky with the means of securing the co-operation of the principal characters in our present undertaking, it is because I am intent on delivering on the operation. I will like us to use such means as would guarantee our returning to Cimmeri with all the money of the National Bank and without the dogs of the cabal on our heels or even privy to the operation before we arrive Cimmeri. My plan is that after a successful recovery exercise, you guys may drink from River Lethe and proceed on a long vacation while I plot the way of a salvation the Grand Master has consecrated me to bring to all humanity. Now that I said this, know that the Grand Master intends to establish a Cimmerian kingdom among all men on earth where they will be free from the quest for money which sight has engendered. What you don't see, you don't desire. What you don't desire you don't look for money to possess. Even when you hear of a desirable thing, it only begins to obsess you when you see it. The eyes therefore are the gateways through which material obsession enters the human soul. When people are obsessed with desires of things of pride, they do anything to get money which acquires all things. And so the Lord Mammon – the unjust god, rules supreme.' He paused for a while, then began to sing:

> There is fire in the wood
> The lord Mammon is the fire in the wood
> Contentment is the wood

Happiness is the water in the pot
The wood is turned to smoke
The water is turned to vapor
Both the smoke and vapor
Are lost in the graves of the air

'To save men from the cruel and evil rule of the Lord Mammon,' the Prince continued talking when he was through with his song, 'the Grand Master has commanded me to establish a Cimmerian kingdom on earth to save men from wanton desires that breed the thirst for money. Once in Cimmeri, men will thirst no more because they will see no more. Whatever memory they still have after the departure of sight, the waters of River Lethe will wipe out.

You will rule with me in the Cimmerian kingdom the Grand Master would establish. But before we bring this kingdom to pass, I need time to meditate and commune with the Grand Master. For me to have time, I need to be free of planning *recoveries*. For me to be free of planning recoveries, we must have a cessation of recoveries. For us to have a cessation of recoveries, we need to have enough money in our vaults. For us to have enough money in our vaults, we need to successfully execute the National Bank recovery project. Our bid to recover money from the National Bank then is the blood of the lamb that will justify all mankind before the Grand Master and entitle it to the coming salvation of Cimmeri.

In this kingdom, the lamb whose blood was shed as a ransom for the remission of sight and memory – the two mortal afflictions of mankind would be the Alpha and Omega, the first and the last, the beginning and the end; the bright morning star that will never suffer an eclipse. You will be the five with the name of the Grand Master written on their foreheads. The five spiritually undefiled and pure as virgins following the lamb wherever he goes. You have been purchased from among the people of the earth as a special offering to the Grand Master and the lamb and no falsehood can be charged against you. You are blameless and will rule with the lamb in Cimmeri.'

Then he went into ventriloquism. This was another thing about the Cimmerian Brotherhood. The final decision on any matter of consequence was always taken by the snake – the Grand Master speaking through the Prince – the Wise Master. Speaking by ventriloquism, the Prince addressed the Brotherhood in the second person plural to underscore the fact that he was the mere voice of a higher authority. On such occasions, his voice sounded drier and thinner. His fellow Cimmerians listened in awe asking no question or in any way interrupting the ventriloquism. Whatever question there was, was reserved for the moment he began talking as the Prince and not as a mere medium.

'Incidentally, this is going to be a job for all of you,' the ventriloquism began. 'It is divided into two phases. The first phase will prominently involve the Prince, Makol, Dikask and Yomoyo. The second phase will involve all of you. With regard to the first phase, I have the names, addresses and other useful information on the three principalities with the combinations of the bank's safes. Starting with Smart the bank manager; he lives at ZT 25 DJ Banex Avenue Sunview Sirama. A widower, Smart beside his watchmen, lives alone with his only child Jerenny. His weakness is Jerenny his six-year-old son. There is nothing Smart will not do if the life of Jerenny is at stake. Mr. Wokolah the bank accountant lives at YK 17 SS Hankam Estate Arrowe Sirama. His weakness is sleepwalking. While he is at it, he is a moving zombie that can be coaxed into saying anything and he can't recall a thing about it in the morning. He lives with his wife and two children who seldom know when he goes on his sleepwalking. Mrs Tamorro, the auditor, lives at AA 115 B Downtown street Nataloh. She lives with her two children Shereme and Toyonika and her steward Kobenih. Her weakness is her husband Lt. Col. Tamorro. Tamorro went for peacekeeping operations in the Darfurian war but did not return with his batch. Though he has not returned, it has not been confirmed he is dead either. All that is known is that he was missing in action. This uncertain state of affairs still sustains Mrs Tamorro's hope in his still being alive although it is more than a year now since his batch returned. Were he then to appear before her, she will bloom with joy and not flee in dread of a ghost. Mrs Tamorro loves her husband with the heart of a teenager. She is said to lack composure before him on account of that love. Even today, after more than two years of their separation, she is said to prefer his memories to the presence of another man. If only Tamorro will appear in Cimmeri and assist you in persuading his wife to part with her combination of the National Bank safes, you would have no problem with her.'

A long pause followed this wishful proposition before the ventriloquism continued. 'Fortunately, however, there is one of you who bears a close resemblance to Tamorro. That man can appear to Mrs Tamorro as her husband and get her combination for you.'

Every man in Cimmeri held his breath to know who among them was about getting the honey laced and fat dripping assignment of going off to Mrs Tamorro.

'That man is Makol. From pictures of Tamorro I have given the Prince, you will see that Makol looks every inch like Tamorro, not only in facial appearance, but in height and weight as well. The only difference between the two men may be that Makol is a shade thinner and older than Tamorro. But since Mrs Tamorro and her husband have been apart for over two years during which Tamorro had seen action, she cannot expect him to be what he was when he went to the warfront. It is that expectation Makol should exploit to your advantage. If there is any other observable difference in physique, Dikask will put away. Whatever differences remain after that, like those relating to voice and mannerisms, Makol, I am confident, would be able to put away at her house. He will have the advantages of a loved husband that was lost but is now found and a sex-starved wife working in his favor. How he is going to skillfully exploit these advantages is solely up to him. That is his role in the first stage. Yomoyo and Dikask are going to take care of Smart. His weakness has been highlighted. How they are going to exploit it is up to them. The case of Wokolah is tricky. The Prince will handle it. How he is going to exploit Wakolah's weakness is up to him. What, however, is not up to anybody is failure. Every Cimmerian involved in this phase must turn in the combination of his victim to the Brotherhood. But for the tricky nature of the Prince's assignment, a time limit would have been fixed for the execution of this phase. But as it is, no such timeframe can be stipulated because Wokolah cannot be precipitated by the Prince to sleepwalk as Yomoyo for example, can hold a gleaming knife to Jerenny's throat to wrest cooperation from Smart. When all the combinations are here, you can then move into phase two. This phase is largely going to be a re-enactment of what you have done several times and so does not require my briefing.'

The Prince heaved a sigh. To his right, somebody coughed; to his left, another nodded his head. Every man was savoring and poising for the role he was going to play in the prelude to this epic robbery.

Chapter Fifteen

Pastor Gojang's bewilderment was how to boot Chiang the Financial Secretary out of the church given his popularity with the flock, which had kept him in the office of financial secretary for five years at a stretch. Head or tail, Chiang would win an election or Gallup Poll in the church any day. Gojang knew this, perhaps more than anybody in the church, including Chiang himself. He then saw that the only way to ease Chiang out was by making him and the flock, which he suspected of complicity in his diabolism know he was unto their game, thereby forcing them to give it up, or in the case of Chiang, leave the church altogether. The ensuing Sunday, he found himself on the pulpit doing that as he thundered:

> But understand
> this that on the
> last days, an evil
> generation shall
> come. For men
> will be lovers of
> themselves,
> avaricious,
> boasters,
> haughty, abusive,
> disobedient to
> parents,
> ungrateful,

irreverent,
without natural
affection,
relentless,
slanderers
uncontrolled,
brutal with no
love for the
good,
treacherous, rash,
conceited, lovers
of pleasure rather
than lovers of
God. While
retaining the
form of piety,
they are strangers
to its powers.
Turn away from
such people.

'These were the words of Saint Paul to the servant of God Timothy!' he cried, flames of fire leaping from his eyes to lick his flock. 'Treachery; yes, double dealings! This is the most damnable sin in the passage we have just read. It was the most damnable sin that Paul cautioned his co-worker in the Lord's vineyard, Timothy to be on guard against. It is the same sin he is telling Give Christ the Glory church to beware today. Treachery; it is the worst sin on earth. With it no other sin was impossible and without it no other sin was possible. The sin of our first parents Adam and Eve was possible with only a tinge of treachery from the serpent. Now see the havoc it has wreaked: condemning the whole of humanity to double death and more – hardship, toil, pain, disaster, you name it. Thanks to treachery. But treachery was not done with humanity; it returned to earth to find a cozy habitation in Judas Iscariot who put it to use to almost frustrate God's second plan for mankind's salvation from the dire consequences produced by the first treachery. Well, he didn't succeed. Just like Old Nick, his master, he only came to ruin by embracing treachery. The treachery in his belly grew too big for him and burst without giving him the joy of even tasting the spaghetti he had prepared with the blood money. Talk of sowing the wind and reaping a whirlwind! That is how it will be with all treacherous persons today,' he said viciously, his eyes engaging those of Chiang in a deadly duel. 'Yes, it is ruin and doom for all the servants of treachery and their fellow conspirators,' he went on, his eyes accusing everybody in the church. 'For the few innocent ones, I implore you to turn away from the harlotry of the treacherous. Turn away and flee, lest treachery overtakes you and ensnares your lives.' Feeling he might be beating about the bush and his flock might not see what he was alluding to, he went closer to hitting the nail on the head. 'Treachery is bad enough when practised in the house of God. It becomes a monster when carried to the house of the devil by men who flaunt themselves as children of God but are committed to the decimation of his house. Men, to use the words of Saint Paul, who retain the form of piety, but are strangers to its powers. Such men we have in abundance in this church and are right here with us as they are every Sunday; even occasionally coming to stand on this pulpit where I stand, as holy men, but who work for the fall of the church in spiritualists' and herbalists' shrines!' he cried with bated breath and thought he saw Chiang squirmed. 'Yes, such men are worse than the devil. For we know the devil as *the old enemy* and steer clear of him. But these men who profess Christ with their lips while their hearts shrink away from him, we embrace to our sorrow. With the devil we know where we stand. With them, we don't. Just when we embrace them as friends, like Brutus, they will deliver the unkindest stab of all.* They remain the Judas we have to perpetually watch out for so as not to fall into the trap Jesus himself fell into. For, if Jesus at the beginning had seen Judas as a Pharisee or Sadducee and not a man who could be a disciple, he wouldn't have fallen into his trap. In this church today as always, there is a Judas laying siege on us all. There is a son of Eli dipping his hand into the container where God's

---

* *The blow which hurts most: Shakespeare's Julius Caesar act III Scene II.*

treasures lie; I mean the church offering, and I have to be wary as must you all,' he delivered what he thought was the knock-out punch and cast his eyes first on Chiang, then on the whole congregation.

Many heads were slumped on their chests leaving only a few standing erect. Among those erect was that of Chiang. Not only was his head erect, there was a contemptuous smile perched on one corner of his lips. Gojang muttered a deadly curse on him, swore vengeance under his breath and took his seat.

Three months after he engaged Chiang and his flock in a duel of wits on the pulpit, the financial position of his church and by extension his financial position took a seat on the knife-edge. If he was previously concerned about having a new car, sending his children abroad for their education and building houses, he now found himself on the breadline thinking only of how to wear respectable clothes and stop the wolves from howling on his doorpost. For the first time, he was thoroughly scared as he set off once more to the world beyond River Kiryanga.

Chapter Sixteen

Josira left Falang the way she met him – abruptly. She then passed through a series of men ending with Heniah - *the second death apostle.* Her first five days in Sirama were spent with Falang who appeared to have lost all interest in her after their first roll in the sack though she gave it all she had while they were at it. The failing therefore was not in her but in Falang who said he was not cut out for a single dame. Once he deceived himself into marriage only to sue and obtain a divorce just into the third month of the marriage. After that, he swore never again to get himself entangled in the suffocating web called marriage. When Josira blew along keen and happy on a big catch, he sulked and fumed after going through her, and wanted out against her in. She shrieked and made scenes swearing to stay put. On the fifth day, he flushed her out of his flat, telling her to go dig out her cousin wherever he was, and stay there too. Once again, she was on the streets hunting for a rich client to bail her out. For a lady of her beauty and youthfulness, such clients were not in short supply in Sirama. They swarmed over her like bees over a man wearing heavily scented perfume. After being tossed about by a cocktail of men she met Heniah in a night club where she had gone with a louse called Sukonu. After getting thoroughly drunk and messed up, Sukonu stumbled out of the club without remembering he came with her, and she too put off to follow him.

As she sat alone at her table nursing a near empty glass of beer in her hand and thinking of where to put up for the night, Heniah staggered to her table and sat down, putting his hand on her shoulder in the process. Though she was drinking, the smell of liquor coming from him made her winced.

'Yeah, baby,' he gibbered, squinting at her, absorbing even in his drunken stupor, her unsettling beauty. 'You certainly get some face,' he went on as if by a supreme effort. 'If your backyard is as good as your frontyard, then I bet you surely have the bees and the wasps after you. Yeah, even the....,' he trailed away, his head withering on his chest to sway to and fro; eyes closed, mouth drooling. By some effort, he was able to maintain a conversation – meaningless though, walked to his car with her and drove away.

In bed, Heniah turned out to be a sow. Where he wobbled under alcohol, he was a girded beast under the excitement of lust. Josira was thoroughly debased and nauseated in his hands that night. Once inside his home, he tore his clothes and hers, threw her on a giant bed and threw himself on her with the violence and savagery of a demented soul. Early in the morning she put on her torn clothes to walk out of his house and his life, but he kindly, and she thought remorsefully, begged her to stay with him. He had in the course of his drunken sleep in the night decided on what to do with her. She was not going to be a passing ship in the night. She was going to be his mistress for a long time to come. He would rent a flat for her where they would express their passions without hindrance. He proceeded to tell her how dearly he loved her and his intention to secure a decent apartment for her on account of his love.

The lump in her throat melted to a happy mist. Heniah might be the devil; but he was a devil that was offering her sustenance and accommodation – two possessions out of station with her privation. Unlike Falang who took what she gave unsparingly and then hoofed her out of his house, Heniah was tucking her into the cozy embrace of accommodation and sustenance. A week later she was living in a tastefully furnished flat in Terrako northwest of Sirama. Her kitchen and wardrobe were well stocked. She swore at Falang and all men with callous minds like him.

For three years, Heniah went on soaking himself in liquor in the daytime and ravishing her at night. Like the Kamba people, Heniah saw love-making as a conquest you have to do your partner in. Foreplay undermines such exploit. Heniah did not indulge in it. As he would be raging inside her, he would be raging outside her, scratching, sometimes biting. Then in one inhuman, desecrating thrust, he would ejaculate, roll off her and drift into a snore – the climax of *the second death* by which he meant intercourse.

Josira sometimes suspected in Heniah's violent sexual antics, a veiled desire to balance his sexual benefits against his financial investments on her. At those periods, she saw a farmer harvesting his crops a hundredfold over what he planted. The next moment, she would make a financial demand calculated to even the scores or even tilt the scales in her favour.

To cope with Heniah's insane disregard of the subtleties of a woman's passion, she at the beginning of their relationship took leave of his intimate presence by dwelling her mind on some flimsy fancy that might have engaged her attention at some time previous to the intercourse. By such petty devices, she reduced herself to an uninterested spectator of the activity-taking place inside her. Occasionally, Heniah did something out of rhythm with his demented ways which brought her to participation in the matter only to drift to her spectator's posture later. To perfect the device to a sublimity that would not suffer her to participate in whatever fell pattern Heniah's sexual orgy tended to, she contrived to pin her eyes on the ceiling of her bedroom observing one day the lie of the ceiling and some other day counting the ridges in the ceiling. Since Heniah saw mating as a means to a *second death* and she was no partaker of that death, why should she be suffered to be involved in it? She became so immersed in her detachment from coition with Heniah that one night Heniah caught her examining her manicure well into his raving mating. The expression on her face was one of total engrossment with the coating on her nails. Heniah inside went limp; Heniah outside slapped her to attention.

'What is the meaning of this?'

'What?'

'Your dereliction of duty.'

'I am always on duty.'

'But you do not attend.'

'I will attend, when you attend to me as to yourself.'

'By attending to you, I will miss *the second death*.'

'If you miss the second death you may have a *third death*.'

'Such demand as you put goes against the promise upon which you accepted me and my attires of refinement. I will not meet it.'

'Then have your *second death* and attend to yourself.'

'Or better still, I withdraw my attires and seek my *second death* in other parts.'

Josira's heart did a somersault. The prospects of being turned over to her lean circumstances were chilling. She veiled her terror in a long-drawn hiss while her mind scampered about for a way out. On the spur of the moment and in the thick of panic she could see no way. Later, her mind hit upon a brilliant and fair way. This way came from a somewhat unexpected quarter. She was wondering what miracle brought

Heniah from his *second death* to life when she remembered the time he went limp was the time all her body went flaccid as a result of her total detachment from his activity. It then meant if she could go along with him while at the same time detaching herself from him, she would not work such a miracle against herself again. Her sensual intelligence told her the only way to attain such duplicity was to cultivate a gigolo alongside Heniah whose sexual rhythm she would follow during intercourse with the latter. In the meantime, she had to deploy such sexual motions as would prevent the reoccurrence of the dreaded miracle.

Her search for a gigolo landed her in the arms of Serho Sangali a young man of eighteen living in Injoko, southwest of Sirama. A loose married woman living in the same quarters with his parents lured Serho Sangali when he was fifteen into the world of sex. The woman's husband, an artisan of some craft, lived in another town with their only daughter and occasionally came on a visit to the wife with the daughter who was between the age of five and six years. Before the woman started making her sexual advances to Serho, he often thought this particular arrangement, which reversed established order of custody of children known to him, strange. But when the woman succeeded in seducing him, he came close to seeing the arrangement as the order that should be. This woman so trained Serho in the art of sexual stimulation of a woman that at the age of seventeen, he could stimulate any woman to a swoon. When Josira blew along, she got more than she bargained for.

She was returning from Atamas where she had gone to buy jewelries from the best jewelry shops when her car without a previous disagreeable sound, jerked, spluttered and stopped. Having no more ideas of motor mechanics beyond turning the key and trotting the throttle, she was bewildered when after turning the ignition key several times, the car refused to start again. She checked the fuel gauge and found the fuel indicator at half tank. She came out and looked forlornly ahead and about her. She saw a vulcanizer not too far from where she stood. She walked to him and inquired of any motor mechanic workshop nearby. The vulcanizer pointed in the direction of her coming. She asked if he wouldn't mind going to call one of the mechanics for her.

'I wouldn't mind if you wouldn't mind giving me something for it,' he said

People and money, she thought. 'I wouldn't mind,' she said.

Like a honey bird, he ran in the direction of her coming and disappeared through a wall of petty kiosks that lined that part of the road. Minutes later, he appeared with a mechanic whose only discernible aspect at the moment were the attire of his craft – a pair of dirty jeans complemented by an overall jacket sullied with engine oil. As he drew near her, the tools of his trade, which he held in his right hand also became discernible. Then she perceived his face. Her heart sank, something somewhere melted but did not flow.   As he drew nearer, her excitement heightened. The motor mechanic moving towards her was a beauty even in his dirty clothes. Of medium height and weight, he carried a beautifully shaped face, rotund cheeks, sensual lips and dreamy eyes. She left other aspects of him to her sensual imagination. The vulcanizer was forgotten.

'Here is the mechanic,' he said, shooting himself into relevance again; 'and madam, your promise.'

'Oh! thank you,' she said and handed two fifty eweka notes to him.

'All these for me?'

She dismissed him with an impatient wave of the hand.

He gamboled away like a monkey answering the call of a mate.

Josira faced the mechanic.

'Yes, madam, what is wrong with the car?'

Instead of listening to him, her eyes were surveying his facial details. The quiver of his lips, the erotic flames in his eyes and the fall of his voice as he spoke merged into an attractive proposal to her. She was yet to answer his question.

'Madam.'

'Yes,' she started, some dizziness attending the interruption of the inclination of her heart.

'What can I do for you?'

'My car. It suddenly stopped; and there is fuel in it.'

They were both standing in front of the car by the open bonnet which she, as was customary with most drivers, had earlier opened though knowing no more what to work on to reactivate the car than to observe the shape of her nose without a mirror. For a while, the mechanic fiddled with some ignition wires near the carburetor then asked her to start the car. On turning the ignition key, the car engine revved into life. Josira's heart instead of leaping for joy like John the Baptist in his mother's womb,* maintained a vacant expression of inattention. She went on holding the ignition key while her right foot hammered the throttle. The car gave a shriek of protest against the assault. The mechanic shouted at her to let go the ignition key, but she turned off the engine instead.

'Anything the matter, Madam?'

'No, I am feeling a bit hot inside.'

'Maybe it is the heat outside.'

She avoided his eyes which seemed to be boring searching lights through her.

'Perhaps, I can drive you home; if home is not far from here.'

'Thank you.' She handed over the key to him.

---

* *When Mary Pregnant with Jesus paid a visit to Elizabeth the wife of Zacharia also pregnant with John the Baptist. John the Baptist still in his mother's womb on hearing Mary's voice leapt for joy: Luke 2:39-40.*

For the first one kilometre of their journey, a thoughtful expression hung over the handsome face of the mechanic like the dark clouds of early morning rain. It drifted and a mischievous gleam flowed in. Josira sitting beside him on the passenger's seat was full of anxious emotions on how to seduce him. Though she could be quite suggestive and compromising with older men, she felt out of station with the suave, handsome young man seated beside her. While still thinking of the best way to go about seducing him, she felt a hand grazing the side of her thigh, first, like the scraping of her clothes, and then, as a fugitive worm. She looked at him. The expression on his face sent her blood tinkling, tinkling. They drove to a cheap hotel nearby where the mechanic who later gave his name as Serho Sangali, expressed his sexual prowess to maximum effect. On the instant, she put him on her pay roll and Heniah was to foot the bill.

After Serho came into her life, romance with Heniah took a dramatic turn for the better. All she did was to fantasize it was Serho and not Heniah that was crossing her and to follow his rhythmic motions. Heniah responded by showering her with money, which she passed over to Serho Sangali. The situation was interesting to her. She was giving Heniah satisfaction by assuming he was Serho and Heniah was giving her huge sums of money assuming she had turned masochist to his rude style and now compliments him with gratifying performances.

Then it happened. Heniah was zapping away at her when she started moaning, 'Serho Sangali, Sangali, Sangali, Serho Sangali.'

Heniah stiffened, then went limp. A brooding cloud hung over his face as he chewed his lips.

'What is the matter?' Josira asked, alarmed by the unexpected

'Who is Serho Sangali?'

Her heart skipped a beat. She could remember calling Serho Sangali's name in the heat of passion. Who was she to say he was? Suddenly she smiled. A smart idea to confound Heniah has crept into her mind.

'Serho Sangali is not a person's name, but your thrusting motions.'

Despite his private knowledge Heniah for a while was perplexed.

Josira savoured a triumph. Then Heniah's private knowledge toppled her whimsical edifice.

'I happen to know Serho Sangali to be my former mechanic,' he said in a low, penetrating voice.

Josira's mind faltered; her castle came collapsing on her skull. No word came from her.

Heniah sensed capitulation. He pronounced his victory in a biting sarcasm. 'I am happy to know I am a mere protégé of Serho Sangali in thrills of *the second death*.' His eyes had narrowed to cold chips of ice that blazed agony. His unprecedented cold, reflective attitude to the present revelation, perhaps more than the revelation itself, discomfited her. On bed, they drifted according to their individual inflammation.

The following day, Heniah seemed to have drifted to a sunny clime. His face gleamed rare vivacity. Josira did not know the terms on which to deal with his present warm attitude any more than she knew how to deal with his previous cold station. In the evening, he took her out on a swing to the hotel he first met her. After drinking himself to a stupor, he looked at her as a drunk would and gibbered, 'slut, I met you here and I leave you here for the fun of all the living Serhos of Sirama. If by any means you stumble near any habitation of mine, you will harvest a whirlwind of justice that knows no mercy.' He walked out of the hotel a venomous anger bestriding his countenance and characterizing his steps like a chameleonic influence. Like the day he picked her, she sat there watching him walked away like Sukonu her mind in a tense state of inactivity.

Seven years after Heniah, she was yet to hook another man with his generous disposition. The lot of them were mostly of Falang's depravity. While they maintained a regularity of patronage, a quintessential existence could be maintained. But when hiccups began to develop, her beautiful looks began to show signs of dereliction. Her sense of tragedy revolved round the fact that her sustenance

was tied to her looks so much that a withering of
her looks meant a withering of her sustenance.
Although her present action of presenting herself
before the mirror might appear to an observer as an
act of masochism, to her it was a way of staring
reality in the face and devising means of reversing
it. It was by her continuous self-examination
before the mirror that she came by her ironical
hope of renaissance.

Chapter Seventeen

A cold weather hung over Sirama in mid harmattan when Pastor Gojang set out once more to the world beyond River Kiryanga, his heart in a riot of anxious emotions. Hatred and anger sat on his chest with a vaunting countenance and a venomous crown. His fiery eyes were blazing eternal damnation and doom for Chiang and whoever was his collaborator in his nefarious activities against the church. How he hoped to death the spiritualist and herbalist yon yonder River Kiryanga would come up with means to counter them kozer for kozer, and eweka for eweka. Such was his hope and anxiety that at one moment, he enjoyed the dualism of a garuda and was transported by air to the world beyond River Kiryanga and from there back to the church carrying the doom of Chiang and his collaborators. Against his flight of fancy, he entered a canoe and was ferried across River Kiryanga to the land beyond – a Willie-o-dreams.

On the other side of the river, a yawning vast land confronted pastor Gojang. The landscape was flat and except for a few trees scattered all over it, there was no other imposing feature. A sunburst from the setting sun striking the falling haze at an oblique angle, created stripes of a rainbow here and there. There was no sign of human life or habitation as far as his eyes could see.

Before him, laid three paths leading to different destinations. Before he left home for the world beyond River Kiryanga, Pastor Gojang did not give two things serious thought: the particular sage he was going to see and the location of his habitation. The world beyond River Kiryanga that had presented itself to his mind was one of narrow habitation of a couple of huts housing the revered sages of all time. To ask anybody for information he had feared would provoke an unhealthy gossip. He decided to do the asking beyond River Kiryanga where he was not known. Now faced with this astronomical emptiness, he was bewildered. He turned round to see if the canoe man would be of help, but he had paddled his canoe almost to the other side of the river. Fear settled in the pit of his stomach like an incubating hen. He had just remembered he had not asked the canoe man whether he was coming back again to his side of the river. The setting sun and the apparent lack of passengers on either side of the river told him that unless the man lives in the world he was heading to, which was unlikely, he would most certainly not come back again that evening. He started perspiring in spite of the cold about him. Not knowing the man's name, he shouted, 'hey man!' But the harmattan wind, which blew towards him carried his shout and wasted it in the vast land behind him. He postponed further action to see what the canoe man would do on reaching the other side of the river.

The man on reaching the other side jumped into the remaining water and went about securing his canoe to the root of a tree on the riverbank – a sure sign he was closing for the day. Gojang's heart sank. But all hope was not lost yet. He would wait for the man to finish securing the canoe, then make a sign for him to come back for them to settle some unfinished business. After securing his canoe, the man stood up, his face towards Pastor Gojang on the other side of the river. Gojang with a child-like faith in the adage that action speaks louder than words, waved at the man beckoning him to come back. But because of the distance and the poor visibility between them, the man could not see any beckoning sign in the outstretched hands of Pastor Gojang. Thinking Gojang was bidding him farewell, he waved back at him and walked hurriedly away to his house. Gojang's shouts went the way of his previous one.

In the face of a night out in the bush under the onslaught of the biting harmattan winds and a possible attack by evil spirits in the eerie world beyond River Kiryanga, Gojang's mission there lost much of its steam. A bush fly flew by his ears. Its buzzing wings sounded like the whistle of a ghost to his haunted sensibilities. Swim, he could not swim. And even if he could, he would be staking too much to dive into the crocodile infested River Kiryanga. From where he stood, the nearest bridge across the river was seven kilometers away. Even in his present predicament, he could see the hand of Chiang. There was no doubt he forgot to arrange with the canoe man to come back for him because he was thinking of how to even scores with Chiang. 'God will judge,' he wept painful tears, which came in torrents of grief, his entire body shaking.

From behind, a hand like the fists of a sow, tapped him. Gojang yelled and lurched forward. But the hand that tapped him, clasped itself firmly on his shoulder frame pulling him back. He fell backward on a hairy chest and passed out.

It was much later that pastor Gojang came to. He looked about him to ascertain where he was. He could see that he was lying on a bed of raffia palm whose bedsheets were straw materials. Near where his feet were, a big corrugated tin stood holding a bush lantern whose flames were throwing grotesque shadows on the wall beyond his feet. The wall itself bore marks of an excavation of ancient origin. What passed for the ceiling of the habitation were palm fronds and defoliated tree branches. Beyond the flames of the lantern, the outline of an old man was discernable from the dancing shadows cast by the flames of the burning lantern. He was knitting something and humming a song under his breath. His neck was craned to the right. From the regularity of the hymn he was humming, he seemed to pay more attention to the business of his nose than of his hands. There appeared to be no other person in the habitation beside the two of them. Gojang wanted to speak to the old man, but fear was tucking him close to the wall. Speaking to the man meant breaking the cover of unconsciousness and he did not know what would come of it. He could recall the firm grip on his shoulder and the hairy chest he encountered as manifestations of strength. Rather than speak to the man, he would pretend to be still unconscious while examining this dungeon for a possible escape route whenever the opportunity presents itself. A yawn came. He stifled it. Ten minutes later, a cough rose from the pit of his throat climbing up to his mouth. He cursed it while trying to suppress it. But the cough, instead of submitting to his oppression, went through the wrong channel of his throat sending him into a spasm of coughing. The old man did not look in his direction or showed any sign of having heard his coughing. He went on knitting and humming with his neck craned at the same angle as before as if nothing had happened. His inattention, instead of comforting Gojang, alarmed him. The old man's inattention meant excessive confidence in his confinement. Five minutes later, the old man, without altering his sitting posture, spoke in a surprisingly booming voice. 'What brought you to Magwante in such an evil hour I met you?'

Gojang's heart smarted under the assault of the voice while his mind whirled round for a reply. 'Where is Magwante?' he asked, finally.

'Magwante is the bank of River Kiryanga I tapped your shoulder. The very spot you stood, is where water and land spirits assemble to discuss their nocturnal activities, and the very hour you stood there is the hour of their meeting. I drew you from there, as a man would pull a chestnut out of fire. If you had stood there a moment longer, you would have been here as one of the living-dead. The spirits of the dead do not tolerate human beings they don't know as they don't tolerate imposing human habitation. That is why every human habitation in the land beyond River Kiryanga is a bunker.'

'You mean I am in a bunker?'

'Yes. That's where you are as all living human beings of this land are. The living-dead when they rise from their graves brook only habitations that are grave-like.'

It then became clear to Pastor Gojang why his cough did not excite the attention of the old man and why he could not see any human habitation on his arrival in this strange world. The man he had thought was an assailant was in fact his benefactor.

'How do I thank you for saving my life?' he asked in a voice full of gratitude.

'By telling me why you came to the land of the living-dead when you are not a seer and upon no invitation of ours the mediums between the living and the dead?'

'I came to seek deliverance from poverty.'

`   'Your mission is a good one. Money is life. But you breached protocol coming the way you did.'

'How was I supposed to have come?'

'Through a seer. A seer communicates with a spiritualist, and a spiritualist with the living-dead. If you must come to this world by yourself, it must be on the recommendation of a seer who would have made the arrangement for your coming with a spiritualist.'

'Now that I suffered the folly of coming the way I did, what assistance can you render me?'

'A seer my mother gave birth to me, and a spiritualist I became by self-exertion. Tonight, at the declension of the moon, I will go to the moving grove to commune with the living-dead to know their mind on your mission. But you will pay for my service. Money is life even in a bunker.'

I will say even in the grave Pastor Gojang thought. I believe when you go to commune with the living dead, they will demand money from you. 'How much am I to pay?' he asked the old man.

'Just a token,' the old man said. 'Five thousand eweka will do.'

A token, and five thousand eweka? Pastor Gojang thought with a sinking heart. Well, compared to what he stood to gain five thousand eweka was a token. But how much did he come with? It was barely over five thousand eweka. Well, the old man can have it. There would be no cause for regret if the old man's communion with the living dead would bring the kind of money he wanted. With pain in his heart, he put his hand inside his underwear and brought out five thousand eweka and gave the old man. After turning for a long time on the bed he was laying, he slept off. The old man who said he was seer and spiritualist went on knitting whatever he was knitting in more or less the same posture.

Towards dawn, Pastor Gojang fell the same threadbare hand that tapped him on the bank of River Kiryanga the previous evening tapping his right leg. He opened his eyes into the engaging stare of the old man.

'It is time for you to go home before the spirits of the living-dead in the air repair to land for the day. The spirits of the living- dead had entrusted me with a secret I will reveal to you as I paddle you across river Kiryanga to the land of the living.'

The light of the bush lantern still burning by his feet fell squarely on the face of the old man. Now Gojang had an opportunity to regard the facial aspect of the old man. From what he could see, the aging process in the man seemed to be concentrated more on his head than on his neck downward. Deep furrows like indentures etched with a quill, cascaded his brows by his temple like withes. His hair was all grey; so his beard which looked unkempt. His lips paled out to a sorry aspect, and his nose looked like the signatures of all his years gone past. The only aspect of his face still retaining a lively appearance were his eyes, which still sparkled with the twinkling gleam of a teenager's. Gojang sat up, his mind at peace with the world around him and the hope within him. All his greedy sensibilities bubbled in anticipation of a bumper future. He held counsel only with the spirit of Achan.*

The old man stepped on a stool nearby and pushed aside the wooden covering that served as the door of his habitation. Standing on the stool, they jumped out of the bunker in turns. On a different bank from the one Gojang first came through, the old man set sail on a small canoe through river Kiryanga. Excitement of pleasing possibilities held Gojang's mind captive. The old man spoke presently. 'The secret the living-dead bid me unravel to you, is the secret wonders of the red mercury. With this ointment and a red mercury, you can invoke all the money you need according to the denominations of eweka you arranged in your room.' He handed to Gojang a small jar containing a liquid substance in it.

Gojang clasped it like a life-jacket.

'Red mercury you can get either from an electric transformer, an airport office or in stores of big hospitals,' the old man continued. 'Only take care you get the original one. There are two ways of knowing the original mercury. When it drops on

---

* *The Isrealite who stole a rope, two hundred silver coins and a bar of gold from things set apart for God: Joshua 7:1-20*

dusty ground, it picks no dust and when it is rubbed in a white handkerchief, it leaves no stain. With your mercury, run a chalk line round your room where you would like the money to stop pouring; then sprinkle the ointment with you in your room. Place various denominations of eweka notes you want to invoke on the floor of your room. Call the name of "Gatemba" eleven times, and money of the denominations you have placed on the floor of your room will keep falling from the roof until it gets to the chalk line. Without the chalk line, the money will keep pouring until it blows off your roof and of couse your lid. When the money stops pouring, sprinkle the mercury on the money. Without sprinkling the mercury on the money, if you touch it, you would disappear with the money never to appear again in the physical. After that, you may consider what further reward an old man like me deserves. Go in peace.'

Chapter Eighteen

It was around 8 pm that Makol chauffeur driven by Jirimi arrived Nataloh one humid evening. It had taken them the better part of two hours to reach the small town that was only about fifty kilometers away from Sirama. It was a tedious journey that left them sore. The road between Sirama and Natalo was a very busy one and it was on account of this fact that they left Sirama early. Though, they knew the busy nature of the road, they were nevertheless exasperated by the slow pace they were forced to crawl. Between the two men, it could be observed that the tedium of the trip was taking its toll more on Jirimi than Makol. Makol whose mind came close to that of the Prince in terms of activity, only stopped thinking and working on the finer details of an assignment after the assignment was over. As they drove from Sirama to Nataloh town on this important mission, his shrewd mind was engrossed with the task of wresting from Mrs Tamorro her combination of the bank's safes without arousing her suspicion. Only occasionally did the humdrum of their locomotion intrude into the serenity of his thoughts. On the other hand, Jirimi whose inert mind even when his hands did not apply themselves to any task did not suffer itself to engage in any form of thought, had to take in all the drudgery of their journey. One moment, he was gyrating on his seat like a huma bird; the next moment, he was cursing the vehicle in front of him as if it had no more right to be on the road than a log of wood. The relative serenity of Makol beside him, instead of calming him, irritated him. On a dangerous bend known as *the Bend of Death,* he swerved left to overtake a tipper loaded with sand only for an orange-loaded lorry to come hurtling down on them from the opposite direction. Makol's only query for his flirtation with death was, 'why Jirimi?'

As his hands battled the steering, his right foot shot out to stamp the brake, but instead marched the throttle while his left foot remained firmly pressed on the clutch. The car squealed with the agony of the oppressed. The lorry driver observing Jirimi's fallout with wits, swerved off the roadway to the shoulder of the road, which luckily was almost as good as the roadway. On the shoulder the lorry driver limped past a baffled Makol and a stupefied Jirimi flinging insults at them.

'May God and the devil escort you to hell!' he spat at them, his face turning dour with anger. 'If congenital imbeciles like you are in a haste to go to hell, must you take me along with you?'

Because of the slow motion the two vehicles moved past each other, the abusive tirade of the lorry driver uttered when the two vehicles drew level, distinctively fell into the ears of Makol and Jirimi. Makol looked at Jirimi and said, 'he is greeting you; won't you answer him?'

The rest of the journey to Nataloh was done with Makol maintaining an indifferent coldness to Jirimi and Jirimi maintaining a resentful indifference to him. Jirimi dropped Makol off at hotel Venderatta and drove back to Sirama to convey the Prince to the venue of his own assignment.

In hotel Venderetta, Makol intended to look once more at Mrs Tamorro's pictures that he had with him and also re-examine his appearance against the pictures. He entered the reception hall and requested to be let a room for an hour if one was available. The receptionist, a fat lady of bad report, rudely told him there was a room, but it would cost a fortune to a fellow like him. Makol needed not ask why *to a fellow like him*, knowing the ragged way he was dressed to present himself to Mrs. Tamorro as Tamorro that had been tossed about by the waves of misfortune. Still, he felt bad as he asked how much it would cost for an hour.

'Five thousand eweka,' she said with an insulting air.

Makol brought out his wallet, spilled its contents before her, then proceeded to count the money the wallet had vomited with the self-importance of the rich. He gave her seven thousand eweka, collected the key to his room and moved off with the dignified air of insolence.

The receptionist's eyes shone with the brilliance of a cat's at the sight of so much money in Makol's wallet, and her hands shook when she discovered he had given her more money than she had charged. For a moment, greed and honesty wrestled one another in her mind. Greed, as Makol had expected, won. When he reached the staircase leading to his room without her calling his attention to the difference in the money, he turned and bellowed to her; 'use the extra two thousand eweka to purchase a toothpaste. Your mouth spouts a plague of odors.'

The receptionist, doubly embarrassed, went pale, her tongue hanging out like that of a panting dog.

Makol's heart lurched. Where had he seen this kind of queer expression before? His mind raced down memory lane and came upon Bolida, Ninatu's friend. The beating of his heart doubled in rapidity and violence. When did she pick up appointment in this second-rate hotel? He last knew her as a sales girl in a Chinese shop in Suleni. He knew the easiest and surest way for him to go back to jail was for Bolida to recognize him. If ever there was a mean woman that loved wreaking people through malicious gossips, Bolida was such a woman. Only twice he had encountered her with Ninatu and on those two occasions, he hated the fell antics she employed in her most cherished pastime – gossips. One moment she was scratching the laps of Ninatu like a cat, pointing at the engagement of an unattending acquaintance and the next moment she was whispering something into Ninatu's ears while throwing furtive and conspiratorial glances about her.

On each of those two occasions, he had queried Ninatu on the spring and persuasion of their friendship and Ninatu had met his queries with, 'can't two gentle women engage in some whimsical mischief now and then?' His present luck was that in none of those two occasions did he speak to Bolida or even in her presence. He was sure if he had such misfortune, a woman with Bolida's catty disposition was one to be trusted to remember voices as surely as faces. Also working in his favor against her perverse abilities were his tattered appearance and her belief in his being still in jail. Turning his back on her who still hung by the counter with that doggish expression roving the pane of the counter, he raced up the stairs to his room. There was no telling what the propensities of a bitch like Bolida could suddenly recall to his harm.

Inside his hotel room, Makol took stock of himself first before taking stock of the room. He dropped his ragamuffin-travelling bag and took a long and thoughtful look at himself in the room's dressing mirror against Tamorro's most recent picture with him. After staring at himself and the picture for about three minutes, he was satisfied that there was no reason he shouldn't pass for Tamorro to Mrs. Tamorro if the picture was a true reflection of Tamorro. In this regard other pictures of Tamorro the Prince gave him were there to assure him further. How the Prince got the pictures, he did not ask, seeing in that nothing spectacular or surprising the Prince had not done before. In physique, the only observable difference between him and Tamorro remained his slight leanness against Tamorro's obesity. This difference he was confident he would be able to exploit to his advantage as the snake had expounded through the Prince. He brought out Mrs. Tamorro's pictures and stared hard at them taking in their minute details. Then, he confronted a trifle that has been disturbing his mind since he recognized Bolida. Earlier, he had thought of burning the pictures in his hotel room and blowing the ashes all over the room. But with Bolida a woman with abundant delight for mischief at the counter, he felt that such an act would be an unwise one with possible dire consequences. To carry the pictures with him into Tamorro's residence, he had long reasoned would be the most stupid and crazy thing to do. Not knowing how and when the Prince came by the pictures, they would be his undoing if they were stolen from Mrs. Tamorro during Tamorro's absence and were found with him by Mrs. Tamorro, or for that matter any of her family members. To leave the pictures inside the hotel room was also not too safe. There was no knowing what chains of reaction they could trigger particularly with a morbid presence like Bolida downstairs. If she subjects the pictures and his presence in the hotel to the consideration of her prying mind that hunts for mischief the way a cat hunts for rats, he was sure she would mew the police in his direction. Deciding to get rid of them somewhere on his way to Mrs Tamorro's residence, he walked out of his hotel room down to the reception hall. At the counter with Bolida were a middle-aged woman and a young man that were not there when Makol first arrived the hotel. As he approached the counter to drop the key of his room, he heard Bolida saying to the middle-aged lady seated to her right, 'What did he say?' The question was an apparent inquiry about something the young man seated further off Bolida had said, which had somehow gone unheard by her.

'Forget about him,' the lady said.

'No, I won't forget about him until I have heard what he said,' Bolida said, earnestly.

Makol grimaced at the obsession of an accomplished prier. Unnoticed by her who was still intent on knowing the gossip that had somehow escaped her ears, he dropped the key on the counter and walked out of the hotel.

Venderetta hotel was not one of those hotels around which taxis milled for passengers. On the contrary, it was passengers that milled for taxis in front of the hotel. Makol moved briskly past a throng of passengers relieving the boredom of waiting for vehicles either by engaging in some casual discussion or pacing about pensively. He was not going to take chances with the snooping presence of a bitch like Bolida.

After putting a reasonable distance between him and the hotel, he stopped and waited for a taxi. Silamatu street by which he stood was a road that taxis plied in a curious manner. For minutes, which sometimes stretched into an hour, no taxi may pass through the street. The next moment a stream of taxis would run through the street like a convoy making irate passengers suspect conspiracy in their manner of plying the street. Makol standing about a hundred meters from the hotel flicked his eyes up and down the street but no taxi was in sight. Up was the hotel he had left and down was the direction he was headed. Thirty minutes passed, still no taxi came. Then a staccato of lights from three taxis flashed through the street raising his hope. But the taxis were coming from the direction of the hotel where many passengers were pacing about in expectation of their arrival. His only chance lay in the areas of the town the passengers were going and the taxis were running. It was not much of a chance in a town like Nataloh having few locations. As he feared, all the three taxis were packed full with passengers when they moved past him. Five minutes later, another taxi was yet to come along. He started regretting his decision to let Jirimi off at the hotel. Though he knew Jirimi had to go back to Sirama to attend to the Prince's part of the assignment, he felt he could have delayed him for thirty minutes without necessarily compromising the Prince's assignment, considering its nature. From his experience in his earlier familiarization visit to Mrs. Tamorro's residence, such a delay would have even helped ease the traffic back to Sirama for Jirimi. In that visit, though he had arrived Nataloh around 4 pm and completed his reconnaissance of Mrs. Tamorro's residence around 5 pm, he did not leave Nataloh town until 9 pm. At that time the road back to Sirama was virtually empty. As he stood considering what to do, something bit him on his scrotum making him release a low, moaning sound of fear and pain. His right hand went to investigate and arrest what has bitten him and it brought out a soldier ant. Almost at once, the lower part of his body from the waist downward, fell under a vicious attack of soldier ants biting him everywhere. Unknown to him, in the course of shifting ground while waiting for a taxi, he had stepped on a line of soldier ants which had climbed up his legs and were still climbing. He jumped, scratched and rubbed, but from the persistence and ubiquitous presence of the ants, he knew from experience that he could only take care of them adequately by removing his trousers. He made for a small tree across the street.

On the other side of the street, the figure of a woman in great haste was drawing rapidly close to the path he would cross on his way to the small tree beyond. Makol did not know what made him look in the direction of the woman, and behold it was Bolida. He nearly bolted back to where he was coming from, but quickly checked the impulse and moved on towards the small tree. By the distance between them and the direction of their steps, it looked like they would meet on the pedestrian lane Bolida was moving. Thinking fast, Makol decided to move fast across her path thereby presenting only the outline of his face to her rather than wait for her to pass thereby yielding the whole of his face to her view by the bright street lights. The execution of this decision brought the two bodies into near collision. A faint scream of fear came from Bolida whose eyes had in the main been fixed to the ground. She looked at Makol and said, 'are you not the same gentleman that left our hotel not too long ago?'

Makol did not say anything. He maintained his haste to end the torment of the soldier ants beyond. Bolida also pursued the direction of her steps with the same rapidity of motion after her momentary alarm. Minutes later, Makol was back on the street without the soldier ants and without the Tamorros' pictures. Using a small torch, he removed virtually all the ants in his trousers, which he had pulled off. He had also checked his body for those taking refuge there. After that, he considered the place a proper place to get rid of the Tamorros' pictures and proceeded to do so by tearing and stuffing them into the hole of a fence block.

Back on the street, he did not wait for more than two minutes when two taxis drove by. He flagged down the first. After twenty minutes of fast driving, he was before the Tamorros' residence. Time then was 9.30 pm. Though a tall fence surrounded the house, Makol had observed in his familiarization visit to the house that it was a fence he could climb over using a rope. But such an action would make him a burglar not Tamorro. So, on this second visit to execute his assignment, he did not even look at the fence as he rapped his knuckles on the irongate and waited for a response. None came. Knitting his knuckles again, he rapped on the irongate louder than before. Seconds later, he could hear a female voice telling somebody to investigate the presence at the gate. He braced up to the demands of his impersonation. Where he stood, his face was well illuminated by the security light at the gate. Moments later, he could hear the metal over the spy-hole being gently shifted; then, he could feel a pecking eye boring into his face. He did not flinch nor try to hide his face. Then shouts of jubilation stabbed the still air of the serene neighborhood.

'Master, master; master is back!' yelled the voice from within. Whoever it was certainly had a voice a cat would envy. Instead of opening the gate, the person sped back into the house shouting, 'madam, madam; master is back!'

Seconds later, several feet shuffled to the gate in a flurry amidst great exhilaration. Hands rendered unsteady by excitement fumbled with the padlock for a moment before throwing the gate open, and Mrs Tamorro swam into Makol's arms crying uncontrollably. Holding her against himself, Makol pushed his way into the house and into the sitting-room and sat down with Mrs Tamorro weeping on his laps. The fangs of his plan had sunk into the ventricles of Mrs Tamorro's distended emotions and he was sure they would draw blood. He said nothing and did nothing while her body shook in fitful sobs releasing the agony of lonely years. Mrs Tamorro's two children, Shereme and Toyonika hung on Makol as children were wont to, shrieking, 'daddy.' The steward Tobenni who had viewed Makol through the spy-hole, hung around pleased by his arrival. He cared for Mrs Tamorro and her family beyond the demands of his office. For months, he had been disturbed by the neurotic wreck Mrs Tamorro was fast turning into on account of her husband's absence and unknown presence.

For sometime, Makol sat saying nothing to anybody. He cut the picture of a man overtaken by the woes of a distressing experience. After a long interval of no one speaking, Mrs Tamorro broke through her feverish sobs and asked, 'oh Peni, what happened? why did you tarry so long?'

'Peni, *the pearl of my eyes*,' Makol murmured the pet expression the Prince said Tamorro addressed his wife by. 'It is a long tearful story,' he said, his voice conveying the right measure of grief and his face a tablet of sorrow. 'My story is one I can only tell in bed after a bath and a good meal. For now, the best I could do was to drag myself into this house.'

'Your voice Peni, your voice. It sounds like the breaking of the wind in mid-harmattan. What happened to it?' Mrs Tamorro whined, striking as a pampered child would, the armrest of the chair Makol sat.

Although Makol half expected observations of these kind, the concentration of passion frightened him.

'And your eyes, they are looking very red,' she said, even more hysterically.

Makol was alarmed. If he does not do something fast, she may soon observe his hair was purple instead of dark or that his nose was stooping instead of sticking. It dawned on him he and the Prince had reckoned more with how Mrs Tamorro's love for her husband would work in his favor without reckoning with how such love could work against him by Mrs Tamorro's detailed knowledge of her husband's intimate features. Now that such oversight was beginning to take its toll on his carefully rehearsed plan, he could see Mrs Tamorro's distended emotions hardening and the fangs of his plan gradually coming off. He has to ram them back before they come off completely. Calling the name of a member of the family recommended itself as a way of outwitting the situation. He preferred calling the name of the steward. The names of the children held dangerous possibilities of pet names which Tamorro might have been in the habit of addressing them by, but which he has not been told by the Prince. He avoided them.

'Tobenni!' he called

'*Ogah*,' the steward who was in the kitchen answered.

'Please, set a bath for me. I am sticky with dirt.' To Mrs Tamorro, he said, 'Peni *the pearl of my eyes*, get hold of yourself, be happy I am back. In bed I will tell you my doleful story.' Saying this, he reclined back and shut his eyes. Mrs Tamorro went into the kitchen to see what the steward was doing. Shereme and Toyonika lay fast asleep on the big cushion chair Makol sat, their tiny limbs in various states of distress.

Makol was getting more relaxed when Mrs Tamorro tapped him on his knee to go and have his bath. He was in the process of sitting up when she raised his cell phone and asked, 'whose cell phone is this?'

Makol's heart skidded off track and his mouth went dry. From the pit of his stomach, he could hear faint rumblings of dysentery. 'How could he have made such a stupid, most uncalled for mistake of entering Mrs Tamorro's residence with his cell phone given the tale of woes he had in mind to tell her of what he had gone through? To make matters worse, the cell phone was a new one. Where could he have gotten money to buy it given his current tattered state? How could he have been feeding the air without feeding himself and without his wife sharing of the feast in the air? Even if it were old, he wouldn't be in a better condition because it was not likely to be the same with that of Tamorro for him to claim it was the cell phone he left home with. How easy it is for a man not to stumble on a mountain, but on a little stone? he thought, wearily. His mind wobbled and soared for a way of outwitting the situation. If he said the cell phone was that of his friend or colleague in the warfront, how was he to explain his possession of it? The best way out of the jam he had placed himself was to feign ignorance of the ownership of the cell phone and hope the children of Mrs Tamorro be not woken up to determine the wherefrom of the phone. In a casual disarming voice, he asked Mrs Tamorro how possible it was for him who had just come in to know who owned which cell phone. 'Why not find out from the kids in the morning? They could have brought it from a neighbor's house or even picked it on the street,' he said, scratching his head and faking a yawn distressed people were wont to.

Then the phone started ringing in Mrs Tamorro's hand. This is it, Makol thought. He had bungled his own part of the prelude to the great robbery by a stupid, most unpardonable oversight. The phone was a camera-fitted phone that beamed out the pictures of all callers whose numbers and pictures had been stored in it. His chance in the jam was that he had stored only few such pictures and numbers in the phone. Indeed, he was yet to store his own picture in it. To his great relief, the phone rang only twice and stopped.

Mrs Tamorro full of the excitement of the return of her husband was overlooking curiosities that ordinarily would have excited her suspicion. 'These children,' she hissed, switching off the phone. 'One day they will see death in the street and carry it home.' She placed the cell phone on a stool and went into the kitchen again.

Makol observed where she placed the phone as he stood up to go to the bathroom, which he had observed, from the movements of the steward, was to his left. Later in bed, after taking a sex-starved Mrs Tamorro through a blissful sexual experience, he told her his story.

'I left Dameta in good will and arrived Darfur with other Dametan military men in good will, at least of God, if not of Omar al-Bashir,' he began. 'Peacekeeping operations began immediately. Within nine months, we were able to bring some level of peace to the war-torn region. However, disaster struck about two days to the departure of my batch back home. Some Sudanese soldiers stole into our camp at night and smuggled out two of our men – my poor self and one Kaltho, while we, including the men that were supposed to be our sentries at that hour, were fast asleep. We woke up to find ourselves drugged and holed-up in a big crate, which was securely locked. From jolts and bumps, we knew we were being driven to some destination in a vehicle. We wailed and yelled at each other to no good and gave up to the certain end of our demise. Our sojourn in that crate was as long and painful as the journey to the destination of our captors, which by our estimation took nine hours of fast driving. When we got to the destination, they pulled out the crate we were locked, dropped it on the ground with the mercy of a rat for a cat and drove away. It was then our real agony and grim struggle for survival began. The crate became intolerably hot and airless. While we were being driven in the vehicle, some air did find its way into the crate giving us some lease of life. While dumped on the ground, no air came in. What came in was a lot of heat that seemed to be eating into the crate from top and bottom. Later, Kaltho my companion discovered that the crate was locked by a combination whose numbers appeared within. So it could be opened if only we knew the combination of numbers that open it. Our cramped brains and sweating hands joggled on various combinations, but nothing came out of them. Then a superstitious idea came to me. Perhaps, the crate would open if I twitch on your combination of the National Bank's safes. Twitching on 297, bang! the crate flew open, and we fell out more than emerge from it.'

'Point of correction,' Mrs Tamorro said, overtaken by grief for her husband. 'My combination is 103 and not 297 as you said.'

'My poor memory,' Makol said, all excitement within, all misery without. Without pausing to savor the bliss of excellent result, he pursued further. He was intent on staying to enjoy what was being offered and leaving without suspicion. 'We found ourselves in the heart of the Sahara Desert with no human soul or vegetation in sight. My companion Kaltho dropped down and wept in the face of the frightening desolation. But I told him weeping was not the way out of the mess we found ourselves, but struggle, courage and faith that we would see ourselves out of it all. I pulled him up and we started trudging on the loose sand of the desert with the forlorn hope of saving ourselves from the claws of painful death that hung over our heads like a canopy of vultures. But in a desert, it is impossible to tell the direction your salvation lies. Still, we trudged on, in that vain hope, that din of will to survive. What was uppermost in our minds was an oasis. If we could chance on one, we stood a chance; without it, our chances melted into the sea of sand that assaulted our sights. By noon of the following day, Kaltho was too weak, hungry and thirsty to go on. He fell down on the hot sand and in a very painful, pitiful voice, told me to go on as the end had come for him. I squatted beside him trying to pump some hope and determination into him, but he was punctured at many places that even if I had succeeded in doing so, such hope and determination would have oozed out of him on the instance. There was nothing I could do to move him beyond that point. So I left him and limped forward, lonely, sorrowful and dispossessed. However, providence came to my rescue by dusk. From a distance, the first living thing I had set my eyes on since I found myself in the desert, loomed into sight. A group of desert birds were circling in the horizon over a spot. My limbs experienced a surge of blood and I moved on a shade faster. I got to the spot to find it was a small oasis and I collapsed on my face beside it. My mouth sunk into the little pool of water in the oasis and drank its water near suffocation. Though very hungry, after drinking the water, I felt little need for food. I fell back on my back and drifted into a nightmarish sleep. Towards dawn, I woke up from my fitful sleep. The nightmares of sleeping while hungry were replaced by those of being awake and hungry. I looked everywhere near and far for food of any kind, but there was none except birds that started circling over the oasis again on the coming of daylight. When I could not find food by looking, I started scratching about the oasis and threw up corpulent sandworms. Without hesitation, I grabbed them and threw them into my famished mouth hardly chewing them well before swallowing.

At this point, Mrs Tamorro's whole being shook with uncontrollable sobs.

'*The pearl of my eyes*, don't cry,' Makol consoled her glibly as he went on. 'For days, I fed on sandworms in the oasis waiting for a miracle or manna to fall from heaven, but neither came. I was not only too hungry and weak to leave the oasis, but was also afraid that I may not happen upon another oasis before help comes in which case I would die of hunger and thirst. Being so scared I was contented to keep the little salvation I had, lest in search of a fat salvation, I find a fat death in the desert. It was on the third day that a bird tired of circling overhead and too thirsty to care, ignored me and alighted on the oasis to have a drink. Though I moved towards it, the bird refused to respect my advance. With the agility of a cat, I pounced on it and wrung off its neck. Its raw meat provided me with my first good meal in four days. Each day I spent in that oasis was a day spent in a cauldron of fire. So scorching was the heat that I took to lying right inside the water of the oasis during the day time. But the water itself sometimes proved too hot for this purpose. After spending one full week in the oasis, I decided to move on to whatever fate had in store for me rather than keep postponing the inevitable. Two days trek brought me to a small village beside a big oasis very much inside the desert. I was overjoyed at the sight of human habitation. I would go to them even if they were cannibals. Death in their hands was preferable to death in the vice grip of thirst and hunger.

'The villagers took me in. For more than a year, I was their common property and as such property was forced to work for them all. I was their hewer of wood as I was their drawer of water. At night, fierce-looking dogs guarded my habitation to prevent my escape from the village. However, four days ago, a Fasodoka military aircraft on a training flight alighted near the village of my captivity and all the villagers who had only seen aircrafts in the air took to their heels. I ran to it and was airborned to the Fasodokan capital and from there back to Dameta; and here I am,' he concluded heaving a pleasant sigh.

'Oh Peni,' Mrs Tamorro clung to him.

Sometime around 7a.m the ensuing day, Makol, after picking his cell phone where Mrs Tamorro placed it the previous night, purportedly left the house to report to office. That was the last time Mrs Tamorro set her eyes on him.

Chapter Nineteen

Yomoyo and Dikask arrived Smart's residence around 8.30 pm. Parking their car some five hundred metres away from the house, the two men walked to the gate. The fence around the house was very high and edged with barbwires. Intertwined with the barbed wires were creeping flowers whose leaves reduced substantially the illumination of the security lights at the gate. Yomoyo and Dikask had carried out a detailed security reconnaissance of the house. From intelligence they gathered, two policemen guarded the house 24 hours of the day. Usually, one of the policemen would be seated in the small cubicle at the gate while the other would be patrolling the large premises of the house. Smart who was an ardent televiewer would be locked up either in the living room or in one of the bedrooms watching television with his only child Jerenny. Based on these findings and Smart's tough character, the two Cimmerians had decided on what to do before leaving Cimmeri.

Silhouetting themselves by the gate, Dikask dashed a pebble against the irongate. It made a light sound and fell to the ground. The policeman by the gate heard the sound but thought nothing of it. Seconds later, Yomoyo dashed another pebble against the irongate creating a sound slightly louder than that made by Dikask. The policeman at the gate again heard the sound and started wondering which foolish children could be playing games by the gate at that hour of the night. Several times in the course of his duty in Smart's house, he had been a spectator to a variety of sports by children living along the street before Smart's residence. If they were not racing down the street on skaters throwing pebbles at each other and trying to dodge their petty missiles, they would be playing some form of ball game. On some of the occasions the children had flung pebbles at each other, some of the pebbles had gone off target and hit the gate of Smart's house. Why should these naughty children be playing games at this hour of the night? he wondered. Shrugging his shoulders, he started humming a tune under his breath. A minute later, Dikask lapped a handful of sand gently against the gate followed by a throw of a tennis ball into the premises.by Yomoyo.

The policeman at the gate was enraged. What foolish games were these spoiled children playing like this in the night? He jumped up and opened the small sidegate into the waiting guns of the two Cimmerians. His mouth fell and his knees buckled.

'Yeah, man,' Dikask whispered into his ears. 'We ain't exactly bad kids, if a guy is ready to flow with us. But if a guy turns foxy, we are some imps, man,' he said, pouting his lips in the manner of a pampered child. 'Though I am a lesser imp, my friend here slings foxes over a cactus; paddy what do you say?' he asked Yomoyo.

'That's it dog,' Yomoyo said with an evil look on his face. 'You take one step out of turn with me, you crumble without a pattern. I am the evil one that roasts the arse of a fox; the limb of Satan that sends the living to limbo. Now dog, turn and let's go in search of your fellow dog inside the house.'

The policeman torn to shreds by fear, turned round to head to the house. Yomoyo after looking up and down the street and seeing no one or vehicle in sight, he wove his murderous hands round the policeman's neck and squeezed with the vicious ferocity of a haunted demon. 'Yo…ur be…ing .gu..ard at this place is one giant step out of turn with me,' he gasped. Dikask stood watching with a wry smile that did not actually touch his lips. The policeman gave a tiny choking sound, then his body sagged. With Dikask in front, gun in firing position, Yomoyo dragged the dead body into the small cabin by the gate. He quickly pulled off the uniform of the dead man, put it on and sat on the wooden bench in front of the cabin which the dead policeman sat before opening the gate to his death. He was waiting for the other policeman. Dikask was in the cabin out of sight. Soon the second policeman appeared rolling his baton in the air while his riffle hung on his left shoulder. Yomoyo sat looking down and making some intricate designs on the sand while perceiving and gauging the approach of the policeman.

'Hey boy, which kind *bagada* artwork you dey do dis night so?' the policeman asked coming to stand in front of Yomoyo.

Yomoyo said nothing, a ploy to keep his identity concealed and possibly bait the policeman to move closer.

'Ah, ah! countryman, wetin dey wori you? Abi you don turn deaf sake of some childish fancy?' he asked bending down to tap Yomoyo on the head. As his hand went down towards Yomoyo, he suddenly realized that the bent human form was not that of his colleague. He sharply withdrew his hand and was making to move away from the crooked figure when Yomoyo's fist flashed at him. He jerked his head side-wards staggering in the process. Yomoyo's fist hit space. The policeman however, did not quite recover his balance as he suddenly groaned and slumped on his face, dead. Dikask had shot him from behind with a silencer fitted gun. Yomoyo sliced off the genitals of the two dead policemen and the two Cimmerians advanced into the premises of the house. They went round the house in search of the exit door their security investigation had informed them about. They found it where they thought it would be. Using a master key, he had crafted for the operation, Dikask gently opened the door and they sneaked into the kitchen. The first thing they saw in the kitchen filled them with joy. A gas cylinder stood some two or three meters away from the exit door. The two men winked at each other mischievously. Dikask locked the door behind him. Yomoyo peeped into the lighted living room and found it empty of residents. He hurled himself onto a deep freezer in the kitchen and lit a wrap of marijuana. Dikask also pulled up a chair and lit his wrap. They were both seated facing the door that led out of the kitchen into the living room. From where they sat, they could hear the faint sounds of a television coming from a bedroom where Smart and his son Jerenny apparently were. After smoking for about three minutes, Yomoyo dropped his wrap, which was only half way burned and stepped on it. Dikask also dropped his and crushed it with his heel. The two men danced a canary, snapped their fingers at each other, then dug their buttocks into each other like entangled dogs and gyrated for a minute or so. Then Dikask broke loose. He pulled off the gas regulator and started pinning down the valve with a pincher to release the gas.

Yomoyo switched off the kitchen light. Soon the gas odor got to Smart and Jerenny in the bedroom and Smart came out to the kitchen to find out what was responsible for the gas-leak. In his wake trod Jerenny. When he got to the living room and saw the kitchen in darkness, he could not remember putting off the kitchen light when he was last there. The marijuana smell that would have warned him of the possible presence of a hostile agency had been overpowered by the gas.

As he stepped into the kitchen, Yomoyo switched on the light.

Both Cimmerians had their guns at the ready. Smart stepped back, but otherwise betrayed no sign of fear. His right hand encircled Jerenny who stood to his right in dreadful agitation. Yomoyo and Dikask prodded both father and son back into the living room impressed by Smart's show of guts.

'Yeah, motherfucker,' Yomoyo said, dangling something from his outstretched hand the character of which Smart was yet to discern. When he did, a terrified scream rang out of his mouth. Yomoyo was dangling the severed genitals of the policemen before him.

'Yeah, creep,' Yomoyo said, enjoying the impression he was making. 'We are here to discuss business and we want your cooperation in that discussion. Your only child Jerenny is our bargaining chip in this deal we want to strike with you. If you give us a good deal, Jerenny would be saved. If you give us a monkey deal, you would be sorry you had a sex life to beget him in the first place. Now we want your combination of the National Bank's safes and the remote control to its doors,' he said yanking off Jerenny from the clutches of Smart. Dikask's gun was trained on Smart's forehead.

Smart stared at Yomoyo and the genitals of the policemen in his left hand, stupefied by the gruesome.

'Your combination and the remote control,' Yomoyo said, his right hand going for Jerenny's genitals.

'051,' Smart said without hesitation. With equal lack of hesitation, he produced the remote control that opened the bank's doors.

From the automatic way the combination fell from Smart's lips, Yomoyo and Dikask knew he was telling the truth. But to maintain their hold on him until the robbery, they took Jerenny with them.

'Creep no monkey business,' Yomoyo said, gagging Jerenny. 'And to ensure there is no monkey deal, we are taking the brat with us. If we confirm you gave us a gentleman's deal, Jerenny will be returned to you hale and hearty. Meanwhile, pal, no word of this business from you to anybody. If you blab on this business, the body of Jerenny would be sent to you in such pieces that you will curse your employers of the National Bank. Words of honor creep.'

'Please, leave Jerenny alone,' Smart cried, pleading with all parts of his body. 'What I gave you is the real thing and I promise I will not say a word to anyone about your visit.'

'Shut up!' Dikask blared at him. To Yomoyo, he said, 'Paddy, tie and gag him up. If he makes any fuss, I will cut off one of Jerenny's ears to tell him we are no bureau-de-change youngsters.' He took hold of one of Jerenny's ears and produced a gleaming knife from his waist.

Smart made no fuss as he was tied and gagged by Yomoyo.

'Remember, any word from you concerning this little affair and …,' Dikask said, making a slaughter gesture with the knife on Jerenny's throat.

Smart nodded his head.

Dikask and Yomoyo walked out of the house with Jerenny struggling and wailing to his bowels while his hapless father shed bitter tears of a man who was losing everything.

Chapter Twenty

From where he stood behind Wakolah's bedroom window, the Prince looked and listened intently into the bedroom. It was 2.45 am by his wristwatch and the third night he had kept vigil over Wakolah from the same position without anything happening. He had made up his mind that night was to be his last in this business. If nothing happens again, he would have to pluck the combination from Wakolah's heart.

Before he started planting himself under Wokolah's bedroom window, he had visited the house one Sunday evening dressed as a Jehovah witness having learned of Wokolah's interest and routine. On that occasion, he met all the family members at home. Wokolah was lying on a long chair in the sitting room reading an issue of *Awake* magazine titled: P*estilence: Will They Ever End*? Other copies of *Awake* magazine lay scattered all over the floor close to the chair he was lying on. Though not a Jehovah witness, the sect enjoyed his sympathy and it was his routine to read the *Awake* magazine every Sunday evening.

The Prince introduced himself as a Jehovah witness and produced several copies of the *Awake* and *Watchtower* magazines in his bag for Wakolah's patronage and possible purchase. After ingratiating himself with Wakolah's bias, the Prince produced an issue of the *Watchtower* magazine titled: *The Coming of the Beast*. After reading passages from the magazine, he took Wakolah on an exciting exploration for the beast to come. The jungle of that exploration was the Bible and the beast they found under the Prince's guide was money the slayer of the earth. *Sight*, according to the Prince, was the dragon on which the beast rode. *Memory* is a small dragon. It turned out by the Prince's exposition that the beast whose coming the Bible was predicting had already arrived in the form of money. He concluded by asserting that pestilence would never end while such beast rules the earth. The fact that the beast and the dragon were already around meant that Jehovah's Kingdom would soon come and therefore every believer should be awake and watchful in his faith. The *Awake* Magazine seeks to wake up unbelievers and to keep believers awake. The *Watchtower* was the tower believers were to watch out for the coming kingdom. After learning what he had come to learn, he left Wakolah mesmerized by the unexpected expositions.

Two days later, he was crouching beneath Wokolah's bedroom window waiting for him to start sleepwalking. On his first visit to the house, he had observed its security provisions were quite inadequate. The fence was too low and the gate was a rickety contraption. The security man at the gate appeared to him as one of those security formalities. If he held any value for the house, the Prince felt such value went only a little beyond that of an usher. In every respect, this security man reminded him of the story of another security man. According to the story, a security man while on duty, took a sleeping pill and went to sleep in his cabin by the gate. Armed robbers came, terrorized his mistress and left with her property, the security man was fast asleep in his cabin. Neighbors drawn to the house in response to the woman's lamentations after the armed robbers had left, joined in her lamentations, the security man was fast asleep. Somebody asked, 'but where is the security man of this house?' Then the woman seemed for the first time to remember she had a security man. Several feet stormed to the gate to find him snoring in deep sleep, his mouth wide open. His mistress in anger poured ice water on him. He told her and a shocked audience that he had taken a sleeping pill.

In a tragic coincidence, the security man in Wakolah's house turned out to be a replica of the one in the story he reminded the Prince of. In all the three nights the Prince came to Wakolah's house pursuant to his assignment, the security man would be in his cabin snoring so loudly that passersby might even think he was inviting robbers to the house.

It was around 3 am in the morning of the third night that things started happening. From where he was crouched, the Prince could hear Wakolah speaking drowsily in the bedroom. He kept on talking for about three minutes then switched on the light. Through the light, the Prince could see his shadow pacing about the room. Using a wire he had inserted in the bedroom window, he drew back the window so that he could see and hear Wakolah more clearly. As he talked in his sleep, he kept moving about the bedroom. When he moved close to the window the Prince was standing by, the Prince wasted no time.

'Butterfly, butterfly,' he said, softly.

'Wakolah said nothing as he moved about the room with a glazy countenance.

'6,6,6 and what numbers?'

Wakolah paused in his movements and mumbled, '713.'

'1,2,3 and what numbers?'

'713,'

'Have a good walk butterfly,' the Prince said; smiled owlishly at Wakolah, and swept out of the house.

Chapter Twenty-One

A week after Josira's decision to regain her beauty by the purse of men, she was on her way to a fanciful, tongue-wagging and miracle-waxing church along Zoronto street in the southern part of Sirama. After several sessions of meditation on how and where to land a man to work the kind of miracle meet for her own type of ailment, the church recommended itself to her as a meet place to land such a man. Perhaps, the first reason the church recommended itself to her was her associating a miracle to the improvement of her socio-economic condition. But on a dispassionate consideration of her past, the church as an alternative assumed a more promising prospect.

She had practically been to all the hotels worthy of that name in Sirama and had pulled all the tricks a lady of her disposition could with men. After all these, she was coming out flat with her purse turned out. If the hotels had failed her, perhaps the church, which had since become a Golconda of sort might not. One quality she counted in favor of the church against the hotels in her business was the trusting and unsuspecting attitude of churchmen compared to the mean and wary dispositions of hotel gadflies. The possibility of marital proposals in a church was not enough disincentive to neutralize her preference.

The particular church she set her mind to ensnare was the Babel Church of Modern Day

Christians located not too far from Gojang's Give Christ the Glory Church. Besides the charming edifice that was the Babel Church of Modern Day Christians, Gojang's Give Christ the Glory Church paled to a frivolous proposal. Outside the Babel church, potted flowers of various colours adorned all the three entrances into the church. They were accentuated for effect by low umbrella trees that were regularly pruned to harmony with their name. Beyond the small forecourt before every entrance into the church, an engaging lawn stretched out to the church boundaries. Three times a week, water sprinklers ran a Cinderella dance on the church lawns exciting the bucolic elements of passersby. Inside the church, beautiful chairs graced the congregational gallery and the altar. The floor on which these chairs stood were covered with an expensive red carpet from wall to wall. Musical instruments ran a riot act in front of the altar. In front of each of the three ministers of the church, lay a small microphone, a small bottle of water and a drinking glass. Three giant air-conditioners stood at perpendicular angles to one another by the walls of the church.

Josira arrived the church during praise-worship and found both men and women in various dancing postures that reminded her of a party of a friend she attended not too long ago. The uncovered heads of women, the loud paintings on the lips of some of them, the pitch of the music and the gyration of some of the worshippers made her to retrace her steps to ascertain if she had not entered the wrong building. The conspicuous signboard of Babel Church of Modern Day Christians was there all right. She re-entered the church and joined the holy samba.

Time for sermon came and the leading minister of the church opened to the book of Isaiah and read: 'And in that day, seven women shall take hold of one man saying, we will eat our own bread and wear our own apparel, only let us be called by thy name, to take away our reproach.'

A pervasive sense of gloom rang from the passage read to settle in Josira's heart like an echo of doom. Every word of the passage was like a pin driven through the balloon of her mission in the church. The whole passage was like a primitive ogre trampling on her perforated mission with the malicious glee of a sadist. She could see her carefully contrived scheme going up in smokes of divine malice, her sense of order invaded by divine sadism.

'Why are the mighty fallen?' she cried.

Whatever was said in church that Sunday, she did not hear. She left the church never to return to listen to another declaration of disaster for her kind.

Chapter Twenty-Two

Pastor Gojang arrived home from the Jericho of River Kiryanga at the hour people living in thrown together neighborhoods with residential premises known in Sirama as *face-me-I-face you* were lining up either for the toilet or the bathroom, depending on the urgency of each to the affected person. Though, not occupying such accommodation, the two-bedroom flat he occupied in Kombe area was hemmed in by such accommodation. As he drew near his house, a frivolous fat woman who lived near his house in *a face-me-I-face-you* premises was squatting behind her compound urinating. The queue for the toilet, which also doubled as the bathroom of her compound was so long that morning that she would have urinated in her clothes if she had to wait for her turn. Faced with such possibility, she had rushed to the back of her compound to relieve her bladders only for Pastor Gojang to happen by.

On seeing the woman, Pastor Gojang attempted to slip quietly past her into his flat. But as he drew closer to her, she suddenly looked up and their eyes locked. Gojang did not know what to do. The woman was well known to him as he was to her. Should he greet her or pretend he had not seen her and move on? He thought it was better not to greet her. She would understand. He diverted his eyes to the other side and moved on. However, contrary to his thinking, the woman while still squatting and urinating, greeted him and even inquired where he was coming from in such an excessively cold morning.

Gojang silently cursed her. But the woman having altered the circumstances by her conduct, he felt he could no longer refuse talking to her without breaching accepted social etiquettes especially regard being had to his standing as a pastor. His mind soared for a reply. When it found one, it was not particularly brilliant. 'I have gone out for a walk,' he said rather off key.

'In this cold weather?'

Gojang cursed her ancestors. 'Yes, in this cold weather,' he said gratingly. He suspected an adverse fate to be working against him this morning. The woman was proving his second disagreement with his fortunes of the day only in one hour of the morning.

The first occurred at Feriwe bus stop popularly known in Sirama as the shit-pool. When he joined a bus from Tekata to Kombe his neighborhood, he had prayed the bus be not obliged to stop at the Feriwe bus stop bordered by a patch of land layabouts excreted in. Though he knew if he sits on the middle row close to the door instead of the remaining seat for one passenger at the back of the bus, he would be forced to come down if a passenger behind him was alighting by the bus stop, he sat near the door. As the bus drew near Feriwe bus stop and its Augean stable, a passenger seated at the back of the bus blared into his ears commanding the bus driver to discharge him by the stinking bus stop. Gojang's heart somersaulted and nausea rose to his mouth. He closed his eyes seething with anger. One hand, two hands tapped him, first softly, then rudely. He was being told to get off for the passenger, whom he thought must be dirt-friendly, to alight. He had to alight for the passenger to alight, or he would be sandwiched between the alighting passenger and the not too clean bus conductor who had merely pushed open the door of the bus and shifted to the left, instead of alighting. Without time to consider which option was better, he impulsively jerked his buttocks to the right, hanging his right leg on the seat fringes, then hurled himself down on a limp. That was when he committed his second sin and nemeses were swift. His left foot encountered something sticky and slippery. He looked down to see what it was and was shocked to find he had landed on human faeces and some of it had spluttered on his trousers. He went about looking for something to clean his trousers even as the driver and other passengers were yelling at him to get on the bus or be shed off. He pleaded for time as he raced towards a small wooden plank toned dark by the harsh elements of the weather. As his left hand shot out to grab the plank, his eyes encountered a shard beetle and almost at once, his eyes opened up to a sea of beetles in different states of activity swarming the mess of a patch land about the bus stop like a maggot infested carcass. He experienced a feeling of being in a beetles' neighborhood. The particular beetle his eyes first encountered was rolling a ball of human faeces *home* when he bent down to pick the wood. It paused in its homeward journey to contemplate him coldly before continuing with its homeward journey with a somewhat contemptuous swagger. His mortification was complete. Feeling wretched, he took the wooden plank and began scraping the affected area of his trousers only to discover instead of cleaning up the trousers, he was besmirching it to his discomfiture. Seeing he was applying a poor solution to a humiliating problem, he moved down to the affected shoe where he recorded remarkable success. Every step he took back to the bus through this labyrinth of human faeces and gleeful beetles at home in rolling mass of human faeces was a measured and watchful step of a man walking a mined field. Now the shameless curiosities of this woman looked set to eclipse his earlier misfortune.

'This is curious,' he heard the woman saying in a meditative tone. 'Your wife had combed the neighborhood this morning as she did the night just ended asking after your whereabouts and here you are just returning from a walk. Wonders shall never end.'

'They will end one day with bitches like you around,' Gojang swore under his breath. To the woman, he did not trust himself to say anything more. His mind was alive with the terrors of his wife's nagging unless he could come up with a plausible explanation of his whereabouts the previous night. A break-down of his car in the bush, which would have sufficed as a good excuse, was unavailing as the car was well parked in his garage. An all-night vigil or an all-night prayer session was equally out of the way as an excuse. No such program had been announced in church. Just when he was about giving up on landing a sound excuse, he found one. The church's harvest was about two weeks off. He would tell her he had stayed the night over in church praying for faithfulness among his flock in the coming harvest. If she was not satisfied with this explanation, it was her business. This decided, he negotiated a turn and entered his flat.

Chapter Twenty-Three

Josira's search for enhancement in alien parts, which ended in a complete fiasco in the Babel Church of Modern Day Christians, at first alienated her from all possible devices she could deploy to the same end. Later, on a sober reflection, the folly of her choice of the church as a ground to ply her trade mocked her wisdom. Quiver birds can only be found in their districts as cattle egrets can only be found with cows. Dip your hand into the sea and you will encounter a fish. Dip it into the scorching sand of the desert and you will find a blistering reception. In the season of growing tails, the rainy season goes for dew and the dry season goes for heat. In the season of growing heads, the rainy season goes for heat while the dry season claims the harmattan. An ashen fate awaits the soul that refuses to go after its kind in the vain hope of surprising life with a new order. Carnal men were only to be found in the riotous theatres of lascivious existence and not in the consecrated sanctuaries of austere life. Her adventure to the church was a stupid mistake she must never repeat.

On the fifth day after her misadventure to the church, she was sitting before an empty table in a third-rate hotel watching the vile gesticulations of drunken men and occasionally picking the low discussions of randy men. Twice, the bar attendant had come to her table to ask what she wanted served, twice she had told him she was not ready yet for anything until the person she was waiting for in the hotel arrives. The truth, however, was that she had no money to pay for any drink. She was also not waiting for anyone. She had come to the hotel to escape the boredom of her room hoping to meet an old acquaintance or a fresh man she could possibly strike a new deal that would give her a new lease of life. So far, none of these was yet to happen.

As her eyes roved over the various groups that gave society to members of the group and occasionally members of a different group, the presence of one man in a group to her left suddenly assumed a prominence of dramatic character. The man, young and sleek, wore a thoughtful look. Though seated in a group of five people, he had for all the time she had been sitting there not uttered a single word yet. The full glass of beer she observed before him when she came in was still full. His facial symmetry worked like a man playing chess in his head. One moment he was in a trance; the next moment he was animated by a brilliant move. As Josira concentrated her gaze on him, he seemed to react to it like an electric shock by jumping up and tapping the shoulder of the man to his right.

'Jonas, can you remember those days in college when Digassi was the students' union president?'

By the frown on Jonas' face, he seemed to remember the days his friend appeared to hold great affections for, but did not care a hood about them, whatever they were. His bottle of beer, which he was nursing affectionately, seemed to be of greater moment to him than any nostalgia of bygone times. He nodded an irritable assent and went back to the more important business of attending to his beer and the lewd discussion going on among other members of the group. But the reflective man was not done with him yet. As he was getting hooked to the bawdy conversation of the other three, the reflective man nudged him again, this time more violently than before. Indeed, but for the close attention he was paying to his beer, it would have tumbled over. He flared up.

'What is the matter with you Gallong? Is an ant biting you? Please, allow me attend to the business of my being here in the first and last place,' Jonas said, heatedly.

Gallong appeared not to have heard him as he said with a rather dreamy countenance, 'Can you still remember any of those historic speeches of Digassi on the rostrum of the Students' Union Secretariat in those college days?'

Jonas shrugged his shoulders in despair. 'Yes, I can remember some of those speeches.'

'Like which one?'

Jonas had expected his answer to rest the matter there. The further inquiry by Gallong seemed to be stretching his patience to a breaking point. 'Well, perhaps, I can't remember any,' he said holding his patience with both hands. 'Neither do I consider them important.'

'Oh, Jonas, you disappoint me,' Gallong said with the expression of a disappointed man. 'How can you forget the memorable words of Digassi on the rostrum of the Students' Union Secretariat the day the state governor of Tokwa visited our campus. Oh Jonas, how can you forget what Digassi said?'

'Well, now that I have forgotten, what can you do about it?' Jonas said on the edge of explosion. 'Comrade Gallong, what can you do about it?'

'I will ram it back into your careless skull; that is what I will do,' Gallong said, excitement of a feverish character on his face. 'And you will watch me do it; and you will listen to me do it.' He rapped his fanned fingers on Jonas head and declared:

> We are determined in
> our anger against the
> decadent social and
> economic order. We are
> committed in our hatred
> and abhorrence of the
> continuous
> pauperization and
> vampirization of the
> mass of our people by

the parasitic, vampiristic and diabolical fiendish capitalists in our midst. We will never fail to feel shabby and angry when assailed by the ugly specter of debasing poverty that daily assaults the lives of our people in a land flowing with milk and honey. We will forever remain scandalized by the crude excesses of our governments in the exploitation and devastation of our people by means of economic and political policies masterminded and tailored-made for that end. This is just the beginning of our struggle. Still, we will like to shout this message loud and clear to the powers that be: that the revolution is coming; it is inevitable; there is nothing anybody can do about it. And when it does come, it will wash the streets of Dameta cleaner than the flood of Noah; it will rid Dameta of the exploitative, vampiristic, redundant, comprador bourgeoisies the way Noah's flood rid this world of the canalized, debauched and merry-making buffoons of his day.

Jonas who had somehow managed to contain his exasperation with Gallong's overbearing obsession with the grandiose speeches of Digassi in their college days curiously seemed to get infected with Gallong's obsession as he rattled on perhaps the most grandiose speech of Digassi of those days.

'Great!' Jonas cried when Gallong seemed to have pulled through. 'How great a memory you have; I couldn't remember a line of that speech.'

'That shows how committed you were to the emancipation of our people.'

'But, do you seriously suppose the emancipation of the common man, wherever he is on the surface of the earth, from the shackles of exploitation of whatever kind can ever be attained through the violent route Digassi advocated?'

Gallong did not give an immediate reply. Instead, he went back to his game of chess in the complex network of his brain and his friend Jonas seemed to be in danger of losing interest in his hang-up by the bored expression that was taking over his face like the weeds of the enemy.* Just when the thin ligature still connecting him with Gallong's obsession was about snapping, Gallong shook his head and pronounced, 'no I don't think so.'

Jonas' heart sank. 'Why don't you think so?'

'Because I suppose a revolution of that character, if it is possible, can only give a temporary reprieve, if at all any, to the oppressed masses. Sooner or later, a new set of vampires will arise using different tactics and unknown routes in their exploitation of the masses. Remember George Orwell's *Animal Farm*, look at Russia; look at even Mao's China; look at Castro's Cuba! My conclusion is that no vermin can scratch the back of another for long unless that other keeps reminding it. No benevolent government can be enthroned and remain so for long except on pains of enforced responsible performance by the populace. Such vigilant statesmanship by the populace is to me the authentic revolution of

---

A parable of Jesus told about the enemy sowing weeds among wheat: Matthew 13:24-30.

today, tomorrow and forever more,' Gallong said with the fanatical zeal of a fundamentalist.

'I think I subscribe to your exposition,' Jonas said in an appreciative voice. 'But, the utopia of it in our God forsaken part of the world chills me like a wet blanket.'

Gallong's face went sallow. It was like the wet blanket Jonas talked of had assumed material existence drenching his proposition. For a while, he lapsed into a turbulent silence, his mind assaulted by the intimidation of a Red Sea.

Jonas watched him closely. There were times he suspected Gallong of mental derangement of a sort. Now all doubt was removed. Gallong was mad.

Finally, in the manner of a man denouncing an abomination, Gallong shook his head. He said quite weakly, 'the subtleties of this revolution lie in its attitudinal character. Once it can take place in the realm of our attitude, our action will fall into place, or what do you think?' he asked, diverting his eyes to Jonas from a distant object he had fixed them while he spoke. But Jonas was no longer with him; he had since ingratiated himself into the society of his bawdy fellows.

Gallong gnashed his teeth. Then as if drawing the curtain on their political discussion, he recited in a solemn voice a popular political soliloquy of Digassi during their college days:

What do you think makes a dog mad?

Sudden accession to too much power.

Is power then a mad dog?
Yes, power is a mad dog.
What then do we do to this mad dog?

Chain it, else it mauls us.

Josira listening to Gallong admired him in every respect save his fraternity with politics. A man she once met with such inclination turned out to be a beast and so she suspected Gallong to be. The close symphony in the sound of the names of the two men exacerbated her growing irritation with Gallong. With almost sublime contempt, she jerked her attention from him to a man that had just sat by her table.

The man seated somewhat adjacent to her was tall and light complexioned. But for his height, he would have been considered fat. His chin bore a tough aspect that gave him the appearance of a movie actor. His eyes pupils had an accentuated yellow background that seemed to blend well with the colour of his skin. His snub nose, which would have disturbed the harmony of his facial looks, was complemented by a pencil lined upper lip. He was handsome in an off-handed way. More important to Josira, he looked like *clouds* from which *rain* would fall; a kind of river Jordan. He seemed to have imported an atmosphere of conviviality not only to her table, but the entire bar of the hotel. To Josira in particular, he affected a warm attitude reserved only for friends or close acquaintances. The bar attendant observing his friendly bearing to Josira wandered to their table about the time Josira was transferring her attention from Gallong to him and inquired whether the man now seated beside her was the friend she was waiting for and what was he to serve them.

Josira was visibly discomfited by circumstances she had not anticipated when she lied about waiting for a friend which now warranted the present inquiry of the bar attendant.

'No, he is not exactly the person I am waiting for,' she said rather peeved by the bar attendant's incessant invasion of her peace, that is if her loneliness and want of means could be peaceful. 'When he arrives, I will tell you. Now will you leave me alone for a moment?'

'Ah, my lady of light,' the man said, his amiability conducing to a congenial aspect. 'I am the one to come; so don't wait for another. And if I am not he, I am meet to fill his office til he comes.'

The last part of his statement was like a soothing balm relieving the embarrassment the first part was prone to. 'Who could this impressive personality be?' she wondered, her heart warming up to him on account of this and on account of weightier reasons.

The bar attendant on his part was happy his punctual sense of duty was about paying off as usual. He was sure the man would order a drink, though he was not the man Josira was waiting for. He did not, for that matter believe for a moment she was waiting for anybody. He had been in the business for long to know her type. The moment she entered the bar and sat down without placing an order, gave her away to him who knew their ways the way he knew his bar room. Part of the reason he frequented her table to demand what she wanted was to harass her out of the bar at the earliest available opportunity if she would not buy anything. But she had her wits about her and had artfully aborted his scheme.

Presently, the man addressed Josira, 'My lady of light, what will you take?'

'Stout,' she said with all the charm and elegance she could invest into that one word.

'Bring two bottles of stout then,' the man said pleased with himself than before. 'And two plates of chicken pepper soup; I trust you will take pepper soup?'

She nodded her head.

After the bar attendant had placed their order on their table and left, the man said to Josira, 'I am Bankas; can I know your name, my lady of light?'

She gave him her adopted name of Heslin.

'Heslin, my lady of light, something tells me we are going to be great friends.'

'Me too.'

Throughout their meals and conversation that evening and thereafter, Bankas did not for one moment take leave of his good manners. Josira out of station with such refinement was sometimes ill at ease in the course of his lively affections. They ended the day in a five-star hotel in a highbrow area of Sirama. There again, Bankas revealed a cultivated aspect that was out of tune with the rude riots of her previous bedmates. Where they were rough, he was tender and where they were selfish, he was altruistic. Where they had no pattern, he had a rhythm. Serho Sangali the gigolo who would have been his rival, lacked the genius of his final delivery. When they left the small hotel, he met her in his GMC jeep to the five-star hotel, she had wondered why a man so well-heeled should condescend to be in the hotel they left. Seeing the man was so well-off, she found herself muttering a quiet prayer to herself – *may he be generous with his purse as he is with his manners*. They parted by midnight with a promise to meet again a fortnight. Back in her room, she counted the money he had given her and found herself richer by one hundred thousand eweka.

She enjoyed an elation of her languorous spirits. 'Who is this man Bankas bailing me from the streets of penury to the corridors of means,' she murmured affectionately caressing her two cheeks with the two wraps of eweka notes.

Chapter Twenty-Four

Time stood at 2.40 a.m one cold Thursday night when the Prince and his Cimmerian brothers struck at the National Bank of Sirama leaving four policemen and five Alsatian dogs dead.

The operation was timed to last twenty-five minutes. It did not last longer. Through intelligence sources, they had found out the location of the switch that electrified the whole bank turning it into a naked live wire. It was hidden somewhere behind the building.

The policemen and the dogs were taken by storm. The operation led by the Prince was electric and precise; each member of the gang playing his role with consummate expertise. Three of the policemen were sitting at the gate chatting drowsily, their guns slung on their shoulders in the least expectation of trouble which before then had never knocked on the bank premises, perhaps because of its adequate security network. The fourth policeman was pacing up and down the street that lay before the bank. The five Alsatian dogs less gregarious were scattered all over the bank's premises.

Four of the Cimmerians arrived from the four cardinal points with Makol approaching the bank from the front, on his hands and knees in a long deep drainage. The other three Cimmerians were also crowding on the bank by more or less similar ways. They had left their vehicles as usual with Jirimi and Kokoto way back in some dark alley.

The first sign of trouble to the three policemen seated at the gate came when their colleague pacing up and down the street gave a faint groan and collapsed on his face. They were shocked into action by the weirdness of it all. Raising him up, they found a knife buried deep in his heart. He was spouting blood like a foul pump. They whirled round each throwing himself flat on the ground. But Makol was a shade faster as bullets from his silencer-fitted gun hit one of them on his chest and the other in his stomach. They both slumped down in hideous heasps. The third man that was farthest from him, managed to fall on the ground with his life, but had his skull ripped open by a stream of bullets from Makol's gun while he was rolling on the ground trying to unsling his gun from his shoulder. All these were in a spate of three seconds. Then the dogs started barking. Their barking was the first sound in the bank's premises since the Cimmerians arrived. Two of the dogs ran towards Makol; one towards Yomoyo, and two towards Dikask. The two dogs that ran towards Makol, ran in a vertical profile forcing him to take them one after the other. His bullets hit the one in front, but it kept running until it got to the edge of the drainage where he was positioned. Then it started spinning round and round in a gyre of death throes. The one behind blundered into it and the two dogs came crashing down on Makol in the drainage. The dying dog fell on his right shoulder knocking off his gun held in that hand, while the other fell on his head. The two dogs bounced off him onto the half-illuminated floor of the drainage; the legs of the dying dog entangled in those of the other. Makol wheeled round in search of his fallen gun, but could not see it in the dark drainage. Then the living dog came flying at him from the rear. Makol's commando instincts were alive and active. He threw himself face down and in the process, his hand fell on the butt of his gun. The dog sailed past him to fall some feet ahead. Backing off, he fired as the dog came flying at him again. Like the first dog, the second dog's attack was not checked by his bullets until it knocked him down on top of the dead body of the first dog. The weight of the dead body of the second dog on him was like tons of gravel poured on him. With a supreme effort, he rolled clear of the dead bodies of the two dogs and climbed out of the drainage to see Yomoyo running towards him.

Dikask and Yomoyo had dispatched the dogs that launched their attack against them and Dikask had even rushed back to fetch the other two Cimmerians and their vehicles.

The electrification of the bank had its nerve center in a small building behind the bank's premises. Yomoyo knew this. After dispatching the dogs, he went to the small building and cut off the current that electrified the bank. With their night vision goggles on, the three Cimmerians moved in with Makol playing the dominant role. Forty-five minutes later, they were safely tucked in Cimmeri with a good chunk of the money in the vaults of the National Bank.

Then the Prince went into transcendent meditation preparatory to his coming out to the world in all his elements.

Chapter Twenty-Five

There were times Pastor Gojang suspected himself of armed robbery or advanced-fee fraud. This thought always came to him after he had finished preaching about hell or the end times, which always ended with a heavy demand for generous offerings. Now, as he sat mourning his inability to secure the mercury the seer and spiritualist said stood between him and becoming rich, he again thought himself an armed robber. What was he and the likes of Pastor Wollia if not petty armed robbers threatening their flocks with hell to get money from them? They were even worse than the street armed robber. For while they hide behind the facade of collecting money from their poor followers to do God's work, the street armed robber has the honesty and decency of declaring who he is on rooftops. Better than them still, the street armed robber has the means of effecting his threat if resisted by his victim. On this score, he felt truly worse off than the street armed-robber. His flock had resisted him on countless occasions without his having the means to enforce his threat. How he wished he were a street armed robber with means to inflict pain and misery on his congregation whom, for all he knew, had been laughing at him outside the church. Indeed, rumor reaching him had it that some demonic members of his church had of late taken to referring to the church as *Give Gojang the Money Church*. Consigning them to the devil, he went on to think of a way out of his financial logjam, now that getting the mercury was becoming a bigger headache than he had thought.

Should he look for a job in one of the outcropping financial institutions in Dameta? If yes, what were his chances? If good, how much would they offer as remuneration? If fat, what were the conditions or terms of service? Against each question, he found himself squirming. His chances, he knew were bleak. The remuneration though good, he felt were not good enough to bring him to level with Wollia, or at least Chiang. He was not even sure he would have the discipline of keeping his fingers off the money of a bank were he to gain employment in one. What then was he to do? Go back to his armed robbery? If so, for what? For the pittance his flock had been cutting for him for a bare existence? 'No!' he cried. 'Never in this country where Mammon is a god!' He must find the mercury no matter the cost.

He had gone to the Electricity Board. He had also gone to the hospital and the airport all to no avail. Though he had made useful contacts in the Electricity Board and the hospital where some staff in these establishments had promised to find the mercury for him in consideration of a good cut for them if he made the money, none of these contacts had yielded results. Their story was always the same; they had no access to red mercury; white mercury though they could give him. He became gravely annoyed when his contact in the Electricity Board tried to pull a fast one on him by giving him a concoction of a red liquid substance as the red mercury. He was excited, but quickly applied one of the tests the seer told him and found it fake. He flung the small bottle the liquid substance was at the man and walked away biting his finger. He never went back to the Electricity Board again. His chances then narrowed to the hospital and the airport. He fancied the hospital more in terms of accessibility.

But the only day his man in the hospital seemed to show interest in his mission was the day he made the promise to help him. Thereafter, his attitude towards him moved from indifference to hostility. He then pleaded with him to tell him where the mercury was kept in the hospital, and it would be his business to dig it out. But even this assistance the man was not prepared to render and in point of fact could not as he did not know of any use for a red mercury in the hospital, least, where it was kept. He became infuriated and called the man an idiot born for poverty. The man was free and generous with his hands and went to work on him. By the time he finished with him, he had a badly battered face and a limp on his right leg to nurse. He went home shocked to his roots and raving mad. At home and in church, it was a tale of armed robbers' attack that was bandied round to explain his condition.

Instead of weakening his thirst for the mercury, his ordeal with the man at the hospital gingered him up for the onerous task of finding the mercury. The stakes were high, he told himself. He must toughen up if he meant to claim them. If the guys he was going to get the red mercury from were toughies, he was going to become one to snatch it from them. With this state of mind, he got set to break into the hospital's store where he imagined the mercury would be to steal it.

However, breaking into the central store of the hospital turned out to be trickier than Pastor Gojang imagined. First, he found out that *breaking into* was not the proper phrase as far as the store was concerned. *Sneaking into* was more like it. The store, like the hospital, was hardly locked at any particular time of the day or night as there was continuous traffic of nurses and attendants to and from it. Sneaking into a place, he soon found to be a lot trickier and dangerous than breaking into it. While a moron may break into a place with astonishing success, a genius may not with all certainty sneak into one and come out unscathed. All these he became aware of to his chagrin. He felt he needed providence on his side to pull off the enterprise he was firmly committed to. He found himself uttering a prayer, the first perhaps outside his church as he set out to the hospital in the late hours of a certain night. By his reasoning, the most convenient time to strike was between 3 am and 4 am when the staff on duty were lethargic and drowsy.

He was dressed as a nurse with heavily painted lips and white high-heeled shoes that threatened to turn every step he took into a somersault. A small white hand bag hung on his left shoulder and the nurse cap which normally sat gingerly at the center of the head, sat comically a little to the east of his verbose head. In all truth, he looked every inch like a lost soul out of hell. He was a bit comfortable when still walking in the shadows of Torongwa dark street, which linked his neighborhood with Baitali high street flooded with street lights. The moment he walked into Baitali street however, he stood out in all the monstrosities of his dressing and outing. Any part of him hidden on Torongwa street found eloquent expression on Baitali street singing for notice. Though no one was on the street to behold him, he was nonetheless abashed. He felt the eyes of the empty street and the streetlights boring derisive holes into him. He could perceive something wicked the way these two were working all to his derision. He could see the light shining more than the sun, tapping men and women in deep slumber to wake up and behold the monstrous phenomenon looming upon the earth surface. The street on its part seemed to have flattened and broadened out to properly yield him up to the light's scornful audience. He shrank back into a lightless, meandering backstreet he knew nothing about. It ended in a cul-de-sac forcing him to retrace his steps back to Baitali street. When he got back to Baitali street, he kept behind the electric poles so that he could avoid the full glare of the light. He also found that keeping behind the poles, he could easily flatten out on the ground if a vehicle were to come through the street which though at that time of the night was unlikely.

All the while he had been out of his house on this mission dressed as he was, two thoughts had occupied his mind either in succession or simultaneously – the thought of getting the mercury and becoming rich and that of failing to get it and getting mixed up with the police or anybody for that matter. If the latter were to happen, he could imagine the splash the press boys would make out of the story of a Reverend gentleman dressed as a nursing sister on a mercury fishing expedition. Even under the best of terms, he hated journalists with an unholy passion. To him, the guys were simply evil by natural inclination and professional rearing, playing up evil with such cheerful gusto in the name of informing and educating. Men whose pens poured out emotional adjectives not necessarily to excite compassion, but simply to enlist the patronage of men's pockets and women's purses. Whenever a thought of his possible brush with such ghastly characters pushed its way into his mind on his way to effecting this mission, he pushed it aside as a thought sponsored by the god of poverty from whom he was fleeing. He could also see the hand of the devil in it; because only he would find glory in the ridicule of a minister of God and so had the best of interests in such a ghastly possibility.

Pastor Gojang would have been expected to dress like a doctor with a stethoscope hanging on his neck and some plain looking spectacle gracefully balanced on his nose, that is, if he wanted to give dramatic effect to his outing as he appeared to. True to that expectation, he had thought so and thought of going as a patient too. Rather surprisingly, however, he did not also consider going as a ward attendant; perhaps out of a settled disdain he had for this category of hospital staff.

Three reasons decided him against dressing as a doctor. First, he felt doctors were so few that the moment he stepped into the hospital and was not recognized as one of its doctors, questions would start flying and so would trouble. But there were many nurses and the chances of not being known were there. Secondly, he felt that while he could confidently put up a professional act as a nurse if required to, he could not do so in the case of a doctor. Thirdly, the kick of dressing, acting and trying to feel like a woman recommended itself to his weird sentiments. It was on this score he opted for a female nurse as against a male nurse who, he also feared, suffered the disadvantage of paucity of numbers with doctors. As for going to the hospital as a patient, he felt reasonably safe, but then his chances of finding the mercury were next to nil. He spurned the option.

When he got to the hospital, time was well past 4 am. The hospital was flooded with light. He flinched. On a long wooden bench in the reception area, two patients who arrived the hospital shortly before him sat impatiently waiting to be attended to. Also, in the reception hall of the hospital, a ward attendant sat scribbling something. Two other ward attendants were cleaning the windows of the reception hall and scrubbing the floor. Gojang cursed himself for not dressing as a ward attendant, which would have been much easier and convenient than getting mixed up with the intricacies of dressing like a nurse. To compound his regret, he felt the very reasons that decided him in favor of nurses against doctors, should have decided him in favor of ward attendants against nurses. As for his sentimental preference of dressing like a female nurse, it had all but withered in the face of reality. He thought of going back home to dress like a ward attendant, but when he considered the additional expenses in money and time such a step entailed, he decided against it. A feeling that he was better disguised as a female nurse finally decided him to go ahead with the mission in his present outing.

He moved slightly deeper into the hospital to be greeted, 'good morning sister,' by a ward attendant who seemed amused by him. Though Pastor Gojang was able to keep a straight face as he mumbled, 'thank you, good morning,' in a feminine voice, his heart quaked.

The ward attendant who had been scribbling on the desk abruptly disengaged herself from the desk and planted herself in front of him. 'Yes, what can I do for you sister?' she asked

Gojang's right leg slipped bringing him down in a heap before the ward attendant who cackled at his fall. One nurse and one other ward attendant rushed into the reception hall from two wards on hearing his fall.

'Yes, what can I do for you?' Gojang heard the ward attendant asking again as he came to his feet pulling down his dress that had ridden up and whirling round in search of the cap that had fallen off his head. He found the cap under a rolling bed, put it on and confronted the ward attendant again.

'I am a new staff here,' he said and hated the sound of his voice which he felt was not feminine enough. If there was anything he didn't give enough thought to in the whole business, it was the sound of his voice which supposed to sound perfectly feminine.

'Unfortunately, I am not aware of any new nurse posted here recently,' the ward attendant with a face suggesting scorn said, making way for the nurse that had just rushed into the reception hall following Gojang's fall. 'Sister Bela, meet Mrs... who?'

Pastor Gojang was incensed. Who was a common ward attendant to subject a whole chief nursing sister like him to the drill this idiot was subjecting him to? Enough was enough.

'Don't be insolent,' he forgot himself and spoke in his manly voice. 'Must you know my name? Isn't it sufficient I am a nurse on transfer to this hospital from Kalkahu hospital? Who are you anyway?'

Pandemonium broke loose as the nurse and ward attendant reeled in uncontrollable laughter holding their sides and swaying according to the jerking of their laughter. Gojang did not immediately get the message. When he did, he turned and ran out of the hospital cutting through the morning air like a knife through cheese. His high-heeled shoes, which would have encumbered his flight had since been abandoned in the hospital's reception hall.

Chapter Twenty-Six

True to his words, the Prince, after the Cimmerians successful robbery of Sirama National Bank, went into transcendent meditation seeking for means to realize what he saw as his messianic mission on earth.

Right from the time he grew into a discerning youth, lack of money had tormented him. He blamed his eyes for the torment. If they had not seen the wealth of others, he would not be under the torment he was. As a child of poor parents, he felt he wouldn't have known the difference between his socio-economic situation and those of others if his eyes had not suffered him to behold the comfort of children from richer homes. He also blamed his memory for the anguish he was going through. If he could not remember how rich others were and how poor he was, he wouldn't have been in the mental affliction he was. He would have been a happier child if his mind had not stored the socio-economic distance between him and others.

As was the case with him, he suspected it to be with others. He suspected the generality of humanity to be afflicted by lack of money because of sight and memory. With these two, money will always be a god that subjects people to all forms of grief and misery. Without eyes seeing money and the mind keeping the memory of the riches of money and miseries of the lack of it, man was beyond poverty. He extended the common saying that what the eyes do not see the heart does not grieve over to what the mind does not remember the heart does not grieve over. His fantasies about himself he extended to all humanity.

When he went into high-street robbery, ingenious propositions on how to dethrone money – an imperial monarch and an unjust god in his view, recommended themselves to his ardent mind in quick succession. The best way to dethrone money he was sure would succeed was to force an eclipse on sight and memory – the stool and staff that sustain the reign of the emperor. Life in a Cimmerian darkness and drinking of water Lethe would achieve the eclipse he wanted. Having achieved salvation for himself and his fellow Cimmerians, he considered it his office to extend the same salvation to the whole humanity still under the tyrannous rule of money. The proposition captured his sense of analogy. Like Jesus who came first for the Jews and later for the entire humanity, he came first for his Cimmerian brothers and then for the whole humanity.

But how was he to bring Cimmeri to the whole of humanity? While it was easy bringing it to a miniature flock like his Cimmerian Brotherhood, it was not so easy with a mass flock scattered all over the surface of the earth. In this enterprise, the sun stood out as his most engaging source of frustration. Like Judas Iscariot, it was at every turn betraying him to a certain death by enervating certainties of failure. His feverish intellect pecked at the burning properties of the sun for a cord to pull them asunder and end the calamity the sun was, but found none. Smarting under the weight of the task, he found the saying that, he who must move the earth, must first find a place to stand on, taunting his mission. Cimmeri for all humanity was a settled impossibility while the sun hangs over humanity. Repeating the phrase, *while the sun hangs over humanity* slowly, his mind became alive with an exciting proposition with pleasing possibilities. The proposition was one that eluded his mind in the first place because of the multitude of the flocks to be saved. Faced with such multitude, his mind had only thought of obliterating the sun rather than eluding it. Having failed to find a way of obliterating the sun, his mind fell back on finding a way of eluding it. This way lay in the means of their present salvation. The sun may resist his messianic mission of a universal Cimmeri on the surface of the earth, it cannot resist it beneath the surface of the earth.

On the instant, he resolved to enlarge the world of his present Cimmeri to a universal Cimmeri to which he would rescue all mankind from the cruel reign of money. This was the first salvation and the first heaven. The second salvation and second heaven would be the drinking of water lethe in Cimmeri. Human beings unfit for these salvations, he would send to the *bay of witches* by which he meant the hereafter. This was to be the first and ultimate damnation – the first and ultimate hell. The proposition excited his sense of analogy. As Christ would come to rapture believers to a heavenly kingdom, he the Prince was coming to sink all humanity by abduction to Cimmeri. And as sinners found unworthy of Christ's paradise would be thrown into hell fire – the second death, he the Prince would send to the *bay of witches* those he found unworthy of his kingdom in Cimmeri. He conceived his salvation even more embracing than the one offered by Christ to only his believers.

'Yes,' he mused quietly to his exultant spirit. 'That night, there shall be two men in one bed; the one shall be taken, and the other shall be left. Two women shall be grinding; the one shall be taken, and the other shall be left. Two men shall be in the field; the one shall be taken, and the other shall be left.'

The Prince smiled that owlish smile only he could. His salvation plan was in full agreement with established divine prophecies. For days, he gloated over the viability of his salvation and its pleasing potentials for humanity.

Chapter Twenty-Seven

Bankas, the man that met Josira's desire for money was no other man than Makol. Bankas was his pet name with women. Gentility of character and generosity of disposition such as he showed Josira, were not his defining traits in human relationships.

For unaccountable reasons, he felt Josira was not just another one night-stand or in the boorish language of Sirama area boys – another link in his chain of sexual conquests. An uncanny spell seemed to flow from her to tame his gravitation towards licentious life. He hallucinated his riotous life spinning round the gravity of her pull and instead of spurning such destabilizing influence on his wanton ways, he was seeking means that would prolong their relationship.

Since he fell out of favor with Ninatu on account of his sexual indiscretion, he went back to his philandering ways. The spell Josira was now casting on him seemed set to reverse his lecherous order again. At a point, he was alarmed by the intensity of his feelings for her, which seemed to brook no opposition from his nomadic sexual life. He was thankful this new obsession was coming at a time it would not constitute a distraction to his cherished business of banditry. On this account, he thanked his good sense that arranged their second meeting to fall within the long lull in the Cimmerians brigandage following the successful robbery of Sirama National Bank. He had felt that a date with her too close to the execution of the Cimmerians most ambitious robbery operation may negatively affect the successful execution of his own part of the robbery. He had therefore fixed the date after the robbery.

The date came. He, who literally counted the minutes to the hour of their appointment was seated in the same hotel of their first meeting five minutes to the appointed hour. While he sipped stout in a small drinking glass, his eyes kept returning to the main door of the hotel. Then she walked in with an alluring grace that excited his imagination. The fairy beauty that walked towards him eclipsed by all proportion his animated hallucination of her based on their previous meeting. Moderately tall, light skinned and oval faced, she sported a wreath of fascinating dimples and a sensual diastema that rolled into a rude beauty that could disturb the vow of chastity of any priest.

Makol tried to compose his riotous emotions to a respectable aspect as he stood up in the manner of a gentleman to draw up a chair for her opposite his. She sat down crossing one leg over the other and then smiled at Makol for the second time on sighting him.

Makol suffered a libidinal riot.

Like any woman of her virtue, Josira had trained herself to read the reaction of men to her feminine charm, and had come to respect her ability to do so with remarkable accuracy, even when some men as Makol tried to hide their true feelings behind a veneer of urbanity. She could see she had made a violent impression on him, and it pleased her exceedingly. She had delayed her coming to make this kind of impression and was happy she made it. She felt justified spending a sizeable chunk of the money he gave her to put up an appearance she was sure would earn her further patronage. Beauty being her congenital possession, she needed only a little varnish to make her gleam like Isis the symbol of divine motherhood in an Egyptian triad.*

'Wow!' Makol howled in genuine excitement. 'I never knew any woman could be this wholesomely beautiful.'

'Is that your way of welcoming a lady that returned your courtesy of loving her?' she said with mischief she was wont to on such occasion.

'Only those short on looks need a reception of the kind you hunger for to attend to their depleted sense of adequacy.'

'I am joyous to be hailed by you.'

'The joy is mine. Baby! What right have you to be this outrageously beautiful? the vulture asked the peacock.'

'Boy! What right have you to be this disturbingly handsome?' the duck asked the eagle.

---

*A Pantheon of Egyptian sun goddesses, made up of, Horus, Osiris and Isis.

'I missed you. I was so impatient for this date,' Makol said.

'Your impatience on this account is pleasing to my ears. The depth of love is sometimes measured by the emotions the absence of the loved object generates. On this score, perhaps, I have suffered more agitations than you. The feelings of a woman in these matters, as in all matters, you know are nearer the surface than those of a man.'

'Which makes it easier for women to lose their love to the chagrin of men,' he said, savoring a smile. 'The mistake women make is that a man cannot be as passionate as a woman if his love goes deeper than superficial. Some men, I can tell you, conceal their lack of love for certain women in a veil of manly mastery of the passions. Check my assertion for proof.

Josira peered into the air in a mocked search, then said, 'I have checked and found you are right; Romeo killed himself as surely as Juliet* did.'

They both laughed.

A week after this meeting, Josira was living in a choice duplex rented by Makol. The duplex was a classic instance of modern furnishing and cost Makol a fortune. Two days after moving into the duplex, a state-of-the-art car was delivered to her in the house by Makol.

Romeo on seeing the drugged form of Juliet, killed himself, and Juliet on waking up later to see the dead body of Romeo, killed herself: Shakespeare's Romeo and Juliet Act IV scene III.

Josira was exultant over what was to her a wonderful streak of providence that had miraculously snatched her from the jaws of privation and dereliction.

'Damn those cleric bastards that prophesied doom for me and other folks of my gender,' she cried. 'It is the daughters of such prophets of doom that will grovel over a man only to be counted worthy of being called by his name, not me, and the beauty that now walks behind and in front of me like guardian angels.' A mischievous whim cooed to her sense of vengeance: 'Go and seduce that jack priest who prophesized your doom, then denounce his prophecy to his shame.' She beamed a treacherous smile only a scarlet woman* could.

The following Sunday, she set out to the Babel Church of Modern Day Christians in her car. Both in clothes and bodily appearance, she was as polished as any lady of means could be. When she got to the location she knew the Babel church was, she was surprised to find the building, which used to be the church was now a town hall. The beautiful lawns that used to create a sort of greenbelt around the church, had been peeled off leaving shallow excavations on the ground. It looked like the new landlords or tenants of the premises, depending on who actually owned the building, were contemplating putting up new

---

* *Babylon the Great; Mother of all prostitutes and obscenities in the world: Rev. 17:5.*

structures where the lawns used to be. A slight wind of irritation coursed through Josira's mind as she sat in her car staring at the erstwhile Babel Church of Modern Day Christians. A little by little, the musical jamboree going on in Give Christ the Glory Church not too far away from the hitherto Babel Church of Modern Day Christians was filtering into her consciousness until it finally assumed an engaging presence in her mind.

'Very well,' she smarted under the sway of the festering music. 'The baboon and the gorilla yelp the same rubbish. If the baboon has left, I will go to the gorilla.' Saying this, she swung her car in the direction of Give Christ the Glory Church.

That Sunday, Pastor Gojang was on the pulpit with the sermon: *The Blessings of a Generous Faith*. The story of Abraham in the Bible, he said was a story of common knowledge to all believers. But why Abraham who was a blessed man became the source of others' blessings he said some people might not know. Abraham's faith was the source of his own blessing; but it was the generosity of his faith that was the source of others' blessings. 'So quick was Abraham to generous faith that before God offered his only begotten son Jesus Christ as sacrifice for the sins of humanity, Abraham had since offered Isaac his own only begotten son as sacrifice to God,' he pontificated. 'A man of the world then may say that Abraham taught God generosity of faith, but we here seated know better than that,' he went on in a rebuking tone. 'Remember the widow of Zarephath!' he cried after a long meditative pause. 'By her generous faith, she fed the man of God – Elijah. Her generous faith was the source of her own blessings and also source of blessings for her only child. The Philippians, whose generous faith attended to Paul's material needs, God attended to their own material needs by a bountiful blessing. The miserly disposition of Ananias and Sapphira was the curse that claimed their lives, and the treasures they had cornered by deception, whose shall they be? Let the miserly continue in the folly of their wisdom. They will surely reap the miserly reward of their planting in Gehanna. He who will eat alone the handful meal in his barrel in fear of a thin death, will certainly find a fat death waiting for him at the end of his meal. But he that will share his handful meal with a man of God in the hope of replenishment will certainly find a fat salvation at the end of his meal. Cast your bread upon the waters and you will find it after so many days.' Pastor Gojang thought he heard somebody whispering where on earth he would find any bread in tricky waters as theirs.

'Never mind the son of the devil,' he pursued. 'Such a one will never come to any good. He who sows sparingly will reap sparingly, and he who sows bountifully will reap bountifully.' Again, Pastor Gojang thought he heard somebody muttering, 'as long as he does not reap from my farm.'

'The infidel,' pastor Gojang resumed. 'One man gives freely what he should give and grows richer and another man withholds what he should give and yet grows poorer. The generous prosper and are satisfied, and those who refreshed others shall be refreshed. People cursed those who hold their grains for higher prices but bless those who sell them at their time of need. Let he that has ears to hear, hear what the Holy Spirit says to the churches.'

He took his seat near Kabelle who had replaced Chiang as the financial secretary of Give Christ the Glory Church. The removal of Chiang as the financial secretary of the church was to Pastor Gojang like crossing the Red Sea beyond which the Promised Land stretched out her hands for an embrace. The money would start pouring in. But a year after Chiang's removal, the financial tables remained firmly turned against him. To compound his predicament, it appeared to him that since his adventure to the world beyond River Kiryanga, the quality of his sermons has been depreciating by the day. Sometimes when preaching, he was scarcely aware of what he was saying and to whom he was saying it. The congregation sometimes appeared to him like a misty mass, which on a sharper focus, would explode into the individuality of his flock.

After ending his sermon and taking his seat on this particular Sunday of Josira's visit, such an explosion seemed to have taken place as his bearing on the congregation became more focused pecking Josira out of the mammoth crowd.

'Who is she?' he whispered to Kabelle sitting by his left.

'Who is who?' Kabelle also asked.

Gojang nearly pointed at Josira, but was forbidden rather belatedly by a quick reflex not to do so, his mind having recognized the grave implications of doing so.

'Never mind,' he said to Kabelle. 'I guess I was carried away by a thought wave.'

Kabelle did not say anything and nothing could be made of the frown that lingered on his face for sometime thereafter.

Gojang's eyes practically remained glued to Josira till the last *amen* in the church that Sunday. One moment, their eyes were locked in a duel; another moment, Gojang would be forced by her flaming eyes that seemed to lick his soul for eternal damnation to look away. From the elevation of the pulpit he sat, he had a fair view of her attire and bodily refinements. In attire and facial beauty, she stood out from the rest of the congregation as a satellite among stars. The jewelry on her hands and neck, he was sure would buy his car if not the entire building of his church and its adornments. The lace material she wore, he couldn't put a price tag because it was beyond his fancy. In many respects, she reminded him of the symbol of Saraswati* which he saw in a Vedic art some months ago. From where he sat like the Buddha on the dawn of nirvana,* he craned and strained his neck to catch a glimpse of her shoes beneath, but was shut out by an array of legs and chair stands that crisscrossed one another on all availing paths to her feet. By the look on his face, it would not be surprising if he placed higher premium on the probable worth of her feet over the impoverished limbs that stood between his eyes and their cynosure. 'If only she would not go the way other rich people had walked into this church only to disappear into thin air,' he muttered a prayer.

Three rows behind Josira's row pastor Gojang's eyes fell on the Prince dressed in a shabby suit that recommended him for participation in a students' rag day. He had come to the church to amuse himself after staying alone for a long time inside the dark world of Cimmeri meditating on the coming salvation for mankind. He was also in church hoping to learn more things about saving people obsessed with money and material well-being.

On sighting him, pastor Gojang's heart sank. 'Where did this ill-luck spring from?' he muttered under his breath. For sure he had never seen him in

<hr>

* *The goddess of knowledge and the consort of Brahma the creator in Hindu mythology. She is dressed in beautiful and aluring atire.*
* *The Buddha on the dawn of enlightenment.*

the church before. What kind of fortune his was to have in the church a becoming lady like Josira with all the happy prospects that went with and a fellow of the slum like the Prince with all the ill that promised. Looking at the Prince with mounting irritation, pastor Gojang wondered if it was not time to start turning away church comers that were undeserving of presence in the Holy Temple on account of the shabbiness of their appearances. After all, Christ himself once used the whip against the soiling of the synagogues by a mob of moneychangers and profiteers. He, Gojang henceforth would no longer tolerate this nonsense, he vowed solemnly. The cane would be applied and applied vehemently on all deserving such chastisement. His eyes fled back to Josira.

Josira basked in her mesmerization of Gojang. She that had thought of luring a minister of God by hard tricks appeared to be luring him by no trick at all. Like the devil who presented himself before God among God's true children,* if Gojang at that moment had asked her, 'from whence cometh thou?' She would have answered him in her heart, 'from going to and fro in the earth and from walking up and down it.'

The last prayer in the church was said and the worshippers poured out of the church from its three entrances. Only pastor Gojang, Josira, the

---

* *Job 1:8.*

Prince and two boys of the boys' brigade were left inside the church.

The Prince, surrounded by an insulting air, stood up and walked to Gojang on the pulpit. He was amused by pastor Gojang's desperation for money. But he was angry he had not learned anything on how to save people such as Gojang's flock. Now walking towards pastor Gojang, he could not say what had prevented him from standing up while Gojang was preaching, telling him to shut up and walking out of the church. Perhaps it was the amusement Gojang provided while preaching that kept him on his seat. But now that amusement was over; he would give the jack priest a piece of his mind. When he reached Gojang on the pulpit, he whispered in penetrating tones into Gojang's ears, 'man, you are a dung beetle on the wrong track. Turn away from chasing the common friend – I mean mammon and face the god of your deluded flock. The common friend is no friend. He will only take you from the parlor of the hell you are now to the bedroom of all hells. There is no water in this path; turn away. Leave mammon alone and come to Cimmeri,' he said in a flurry and stood looking at Gojang, contemptuously.

There was no response from Gojang. Too shocked by the brashness of the assault and the insulting aura of the man that committed it, he only sat gaping at the prince who at that moment was expecting him to take his Bible and follow him to

Cimmeri. After waiting for a moment that was beginning to attract the attention of the two boys of the boys-brigade, the Prince hissed loudly and swept out of the church.

Josira sitting on her seat like an abject Shinto* devotee pretending to be reading her Bible wondered who the hell the Prince was. Somehow, she couldn't place him as a regular church member and could not also place him as an outsider considering the confidence he walked up to pastor Gojang and whispered into his ears. But if he was a church member, why was Gojang looking so distant and apparently offended by his presence and whatever he was telling him. And then there was the uneasy silence after he had finished speaking to Gojang. What of the loud hiss? Well, well that was their problem. It did not in the slightest degree affect her mission in the church that day.

Gojang though gravely irritated by the Prince soon dismissed him as one of those weird characters one comes across in life. Josira was too important a prospect to be passed off because of annoyance by an accursed freak like the Prince. As soon as the Prince left the church, he walked towards Josira as a minister of God would and asked rather too kindly, 'sister, I hope there is no problem?'

A Japanese religion that means way of the gods. It mainly consists of worship of ancestral spirits. Shinto worshippers at worship cut an object picture.

'There is a small problem,' she said in the humble voice of a supplicant.

'Perhaps we should go into the counseling room to discuss it?'

'No problem.'

Pastor Gojang since accosting Josira had surprisingly comported himself better than when he sat staring at her during church proceedings. She who had perfected the art of seeing through the pretensions of lecherous men peeped through Gojang's composure to see if he was pulling one of such stunts debauched men were wont to, but saw nothing. On that score, Gojang was himself inside as he was himself outside. His expectation of money from her, she could not see because the only thing men had sought from her was sex. Rather baffled by Gojang's indifference to her sexual appeal, her earlier fancy that she might not be obliged to apply hard tricks to compromise Pastor Gojang, withered like mist before the rising sun.

Seated inside the counseling room opposite Pastor Gojang, she committed herself to tackling the pastor in his own field. Opening the book of Acts of the Apostles, she read the verse: 'Jesus I know, and Paul I know, but who are you?' Abruptly, she looked up and said to Pastor Gojang, 'anytime I read this verse of the Bible, my spirit does not seem to get at its hidden meaning. Can you explain its hidden meaning to me?'

Even as she spoke, her probing eyes were busy assigning value to the shades of expression pursuing one another on Pastor Gojang's face like athletes in a relay race.

For an agonizing moment, Gojang stared at the challenge thrown at him with the horror of a man being invited by a snake charmer to take hold of a writhing snake in one of those macabre shows of snake charmers. Once he opened his mouth, but no word came out.

Josira observed his mortification and stabbed him with her mission: 'Do you think a time will ever come when seven women will line up for one man only to be counted worthy of being called by his name?'

Pastor Gojang whose mind was spinning round in a whirlwind of shame and embarrassment murmured, 'no such time will ever come.'

'Sadistic maggots of false prophecies,' Josira hissed to herself.

Pastor Gojang only about emerging from his delirium did not hear her. As he hit the threshold of sanity, Josira was already by his side embracing him.

Something stirred in Gojang's valley and his weak protests dissolved into a moan. On the floor of the counseling room, Pastor Gojang ate the forbidden fruit.

Chapter Twenty-Eight

For three days, the Prince remained holed-up in the dark world of Cimmeri brooding over the means he had resolved to dethrone money – bringing Cimmeri to the generality of humanity. Whichever way he looked at the matter he could not find better means of achieving his keenly felt destiny than by the means he had elected to. Those he would abduct to Cimmeri would add to the number of his *angels* that would *rapture* more people to Cimmeri. At intervals, he amused himself with the grand oration he would deliver to captive humanity on the occasion of the universal coming of Cimmeri:

> I, the Prince, the avatar of
> your creator has heard the
> cry of my people which
> had come down to me in
> Cimmeri. I have come out
> to see which fox is among
> my pigeons. Lo, I behold
> the plagues of sight and
> memory – two plagues
> woeful than the twelve
> plagues of Egypt,
> ravaging my people. I see
> the two plagues of sight
> and memory breeding
> *pride* which has

established the rule of the Lord Mammon on earth. The Lord Mammon has thrown my people into a war for wealth. Mammon has turned each against all and all against each. Son is shoving father aside to reach Mammon and mother is elbowing daughter to reach Mammon. Slavery, colonialism and globalization which impoverished many were all caused by the Lord Mammon.

If sight and memory go, pride will go. If *pride* goes, the Lord Mammon and his tyrannical rule will be no more. When the reason for a thing ceases, the thing ceases with the reason. I, the Prince, is here to end the tyranny of the Lord Mammon by withdrawing sight, memory and *pride* the trinity on which his reign is founded, the three stones making the hearth on which the pot of the Lord Mammon is cooking food for only a few. With the inane justification of Cimmeri and the amnesic absolution of the waters of river Lethe, my fellow Cimmerians, all men on earth are about to enjoy the eclipse of the final Passover.

Musing over this oration, an imperial passion whispered to the Prince's sense of the imminently desirable. He called a meeting of his fellow Cimmerian brothers. After briefing them on the coming salvation of mankind in the usual ventriloquism, he waited for their acquiescence in the scheme. One after the other, the Cimmerian brothers expressed support for the Prince's salvation plan until it was the turn of Makol to speak. Other Cimmerians, like the children of Israel before Mount Nebo,* waited in vain for Makol to say something in league with their general consensus, but no word came from him.

---

* *When prophet Moses who was leading the Israelites from Egypt to the promised land of Canaan, climbed mount Nebo to take a view of the promised land, his people waited in vain for him, but he never came down from the mountain. Deut. 34:1-8*

Makol whose thoughts had carried him far away from them into the laps of Josira did not even know they were waiting for him. Relishing the genius of her passion and his love for her, he was contemplating what he could not even with Ninatu his first love – marriage. Only marriage with Josira would spare him the fear of losing her to other men. It turned out that while other Cimmerians were discussing the coming of a universal salvation, Makol was thinking of his libidinal salvation.

In all meetings of the Cimmerian Brotherhood, Makol usually lay prostrate immediately to the right of the Prince as the undeclared second mastermind in Cimmeri. When no word came from him on this occasion, the Prince whose head lay by his feet pulled his right thumb. Makol thinking the snake was snapping at his thumb, kicked out with a loud shriek. The heel of his foot travelling only a few inches encountered the lower jaw of the Prince. The jarring impact of the collision set Makol's teeth on edge and the Prince's dentistry loose. In the dark world of Cimmeri, the Prince could only feel the blood gushing out of his mouth and one tooth that had completely come off. His cry of agony sounded like the caterwauling of a cat on the prowl for preys.

This accident brought to the fore the discipline of the Cimmerian brothers which had seen them through the most exerting robbery operations over the years of their coming together. No Cimmerian left his prostrate position to commiserate with the Prince and none thought of putting on his night vision goggles to know the source and character of his harm, though they suspected it to be connected with the shrieking of Makol. The Prince, on his part, was still intent on knowing what Makol's position was on the matter in handling. He crawled to a bowl containing a liquid substance kept by him at the centre of a circle and filled his mouth with it. The tormenting pain immediately subsided. He crawled back to his position and said quietly, 'we are still waiting.'

'For Heslin?' Makol who now mingled thoughts of Josira with the mishap he had caused, blurted out impulsively.

'Who is Heslin?' the Prince asked, all his mean elements alive and haughty. Other Cimmerians ground their teeth at the palpable derangement of order in Cimmeri.

'Damn her,' Makol muttered.

'Who is she?' the Prince repeated.

'Never mind who she is,' Makol said with a lot of warmth. 'She is my personal affair and I intend to take care of her my ruthless way.' He had warned himself to handle the matter with the guile of a conman if he did not want the Prince to lay his paws on Josira, and he would give anything to spare her his presence. This attitude, however, took nothing of his decision just arrived at – to get married to Josira and break away from the Brotherhood.

But the Prince was too sharp to fall for such gimmick. He saw through it like a pellucid wear and set his own ploy upon it.

'I know you of all Cimmerians can't afford to act Judas at the eleventh hour,' he said in the smooth manner of a courting teenager. 'Handle that little business the smart way I trust you. On the matter at hand, what do you say?'

Makol, who by the stroke of his intellect, had been able to piece together the various strands of the discussion that had intruded into the spelling melody from Josira's romantic flute, which, like that of Durga Kali,* had taken his soul captive, had a ready answer for the Prince and the other Cimmerians on his position on the matter.

'I acquiesce to the collective will,' he said simply. Within him, his mind was alive with propositions of his own personal plans. Like the Prince, the Prince's cunning did not deceive him. He knew the Prince's mean instincts once excited the manner he had excited them, knew no rest until they reached the bottom of the matter. Other Cimmerians were with him in not being taken in by the Prince's feigned pacification. If anybody in Cimmeri was deceived by the Prince's seeming pacification, it must be Jirimi or Kokoto.

---

* *Wife of Siva in Hindu mythology who plays a mesmerizing tune on a flute.*

The meeting dispersed. Seven weeks later, the bunker of Cimmeri was sufficiently enlarged by a dredging machine the Prince had acquired for the purpose. Then the Cimmerians took to the field in the abduction of people. Today a husband was mourning a missing wife, the other day, a mother wept for a missing son. As the Prince had prophesied: two women were grinding, one was taken and the other was left; two men were in the field, one was taken and the other left.

Like his concoction of the water of River Lethe, the Prince concocted a trigger-gas that induced instant coma the moment air carrying it was inhaled. The use of this gas made it possible for the Cimmerians to fulfill the Prince's prophecy of the rapture by *taking one and leaving one*. Whenever they went out to abduct people in fulfillment of the prophecy of the rapture, they went with the gas in a sprayer can, which they sprayed at their victims. During the unconsciousness of their victims, the Brotherhood decided who shall be taken to their kingdom and who shall be left to suffer the 1,000 years of persecution by the devil in the cruel world of mammon.

Beside the use of trigger-gas, the Cimmerians employed various other means of abducting people to their Cimmerian world. Often, the mode of abduction was determined by the character of the abductee and his circumstances. While the gas was more likely to be used against persons whose circumstances fit the prophecy of *two being in bed or grinding, one taken, and the other left*, violence and treachery were more likely to be employed against persons who did not fit into such circumstances. Within two weeks, the dark world of Cimmeri was bustling with an assorted crowd vegetating under a kind of salvation.

Among the abductees in Cimmeri were Imam Balako, Senator Ajanye and Justice Henema. Imam Balako was abducted, or perhaps, more appropriately as meet his circumstances, enchanted on his way to a marabout to receive further direction on a money-making ritual the marabout was seeing him through and also to get interpretation from the marabout of a dream he had the previous night. The ritual consisted of making love to a donkey, taking a drop of his semen and burying it in a cemetery together with a chaplet and amulets the marabout had given him. The marabout had assured him once these were done, he would be sitting on a money-spinning hub. He had already carried out these instructions of the marabout. His present trip to the marabout was to receive further direction on the rituals and an interpretation of a dream he had the previous night.

He had dreamed he was returning from the marabout's shrine carrying a basket full of money when the earth opened and swallowed him up. Inside the womb of the earth, he met the Mahdi dressed in a white toga. From the Mahdi's toga flowed a million stars to form a dazzling crown of honor over his head while the Mahdi was hailing him as the chief priest in the shrine of *nuqud*. He, observing the crown of glory the stars had formed above his head and hearing the praises of the Mahdi, started laughing and nodding his head in satisfaction with his grandeur. He woke up laughing to find himself in his blighted habitation. A slight wind of irritation coursed through his mind to be cheered up by a recollection of the uncanny way his dreams sometimes came to pass. He once dreamed the President of Dameta invited him to a banquet in the presidential castle and two weeks later, he with other religious leaders were invited to the presidential castle by the President to pray for the continuous docility of the people however they were oppressed.

With pleasing memories of the fulfillment of this dream, Imam Balako left his house on the day of his abduction or enchantment by the Prince with high expectations of material fulfillment of his present dream in aspects that would tend to his material elevation.

Trekking on a small blind path that led to the marabout's shrine, he bent down near a thicket beside the path to remove a sharp twig that had pierced through the soft sole of his footwear. Then the Prince appeared to him from behind the thicket wearing a *burqa*. His mouth was mumbling something Imam Balako could not hear and his hands were spread out like the wings of a rising angel. Memories of his dream, which had not been far from his thoughts, flooded his mind taking him captive. He fell down on his knees and commenced the Salat. It was in this hypnotic state the Prince took him to Cimmeri.

In Cimmeri, he met Senator Ajanye and Justice Henema who arrived the bunker a day earlier. Senator Ajanye and Justice Henema were abducted together in Senator Ajanye's house. Yomoyo and Dikask had gone to abduct Senator Ajanye who had gained notoriety as a loud-mouth in the government of president Majenka only to meet Justice Henema discussing a political case pending in Justice Henema's court. From much of the conversation they could pick from their hide-out under the balcony the two men sat discussing. Dikask and Yomoyo gathered Ajanye had actually sent for Justice Henema to brief him on the progress of the case and how far he had been conducting it in line with agreed objectives between him and the government. When the discussion got round to the consideration for Justice Henema tilting the scale of justice in favor of Majenka, Dikask and Yomoyo could distinctively hear Justice Henema complaining the government was slow in performing its part of the bargain which included award of oil blocks to him and his front-men. 'You senators keep belching while we are yawning on the bench,' they heard Justice Henema saying.

'Hmmm…. I don't know about that,' they heard Senator Ajanye smirking. 'I think somebody

is forgetting something here. Who it is, I don't
know. But I suppose somebody on the bench is
reserved for yawning and a Senator in the court of
dissension should not be begrudged by such a one.
We all made our choices. Why then should the
vulture begrudge the hawk her lightness of limbs?'

'You have a point,' Justice Henema said.
'All the same, I am tired of seeing *yo-yo* boys in
business upstaging me in our town meetings
because they are home with big cars and fat
wallets that meet the aspirations of our greedy
chief for all the sons of his domain particularly
those of them in Sirama, which in his warped
imagination, is a Tom Tiddler's ground of some
sort. The sight and memory of...'

'No more sights, no more memories and no
more mammon,' Dikask said emerging from their
hideout. His gun was pointing at Justice Henema
while Yomoyo had his trained on Senator Ajanye.
'Cimmeri and water Lethe are here to deliver you
from the miseries of sight, memory and money,' he
said, enjoying the looks of horror that had
overtaken the faces of the two men about to suffer
the eclipse of the final passover. From there, they
were bundled into the car that brought the two
Cimmerians and taken to Cimmeri.

As soon as an abductee arrived Cimmeri,
depending on his loyalty as determined by the
Prince, he was either fed with water Lethe to last
him a life-time or was co-opted into the
Cimmerian Brotherhood to help in the abudction

of others. Salvation meet only for a world under the tyranny of the Lord Mammon was spreading fast in Dameta and was to spread to the four corners of the earth. In Sirama where it had flagged off, the fear of the unknown shone in people's faces like the pit of hell.

Chapter Twenty-Nine

Beyond the weird fancy of a woman, the attachment of Josira to Pastor Gojang was difficult to account for, even to herself. When she first set out to take vengeance on a man of God for his prophecy of doom on women, she did not harbor thoughts of a long relationship. When she did not find the man she was seeking and ended up with Pastor Gojang, her spirit of vengeance, instead of dissipating, seemed to go beyond man to God himself. She was angry with God for the poverty she was born into and for his complicity in her abuse by men which he nearly turned to her derision by his one man, seven women prophecy. Since she had outwitted him in his game of sadism, it became her place to continuously mock his thwarted sadism. Perhaps, for this end, she clung tightly to Pastor Gojang as the means. The counseling room of Give Christ the Glory Church became their love nest where she was sure to be found almost on a daily basis. Only on rare occasions did she allow Pastor Gojang make love to her outside the counseling room. Having discovered pastor Gojang's real weakness to be money, she getting a lot of money from Makol, passed some of it to him as a means of consolidating her hold on him.

On his part, Pastor Gojang meeting in an unlikely quarter the desire of his heart, which had taken him to bizarre lengths, gave no thought to any consideration, but the glorification of a pleasing eventuality by whatever agency. Full of gratitude to God for sending manna to him, though in Egypt instead of the promised land of Canaan, he prayed that God should keep him under the tree of Josira's generosity, which had fetched him a new car. But if the tree was about to fall, he should take him and spread him under another generous tree.

Between Josira and Makol, matters had not been progressing as Makol would have liked. By all showing, he loved Josira more than she loved him. While he pressed for an immediate marriage, which he had for reasons only known to him staked his desertion of the Cimmerian Brotherhood on, Josira loving him less, strained for a distant marriage, if at all any. She had by reason of her mother's disappointment with that institution, sworn to spare herself its ordeal, and she was not about changing her mind on account of any man. She knew she had sunk a hook into Makol. Each day, she watched the hook sinking deeper and deeper into Makol's heart. She was jubilant. The men who had abused her were men like Makol. They all belonged to the same tribe of heartless leeches. So, let Makol labour to his own impoverishment. For her, she would continue to spin him and that *Sabbath fellow* round her whimsical fingers.

Then it happened. One of those rare coincidences that only the office of providence can contrive occurred to gather the worshippers of Mammon and the Messiah of mankind from the oppressive rule of Mammon in Josira's court. Pastor Gojang was the first to arrive. He got to Josira's apartment around 8pm on the fateful day of his rendezvous with the other worshippers and the Messiah. He was actually not supposed to go to her house that day by the arrangement between the two. Josira was to meet him in the counseling room by 4pm to give him some money she had promised him. After waiting for more than three hours without her turning up, he set out for her house. He got to the house to find her playing a computer game. She had completely forgotten about the appointment. He was enraged. But the consequences of giving vent to his anger overwhelmed the benefits. He joined her in the game. Unconscious of time, the wall clock in the master's bedroom chimed 10pm without their knowing it. Then Makol arrived as quietly as a ghost.

His car had developed electrical faults about three hundred meters away from the house. Not having light to check what the matter was, he had rushed to the house to get one. On sighting Pastor Gojang's car parked in front of Josira's apartment, his walloping steps alternated into the steps of a predator. Gently opening the door with his spare key, he sneaked into the living room not bothering to close the door for fear it might make a creaking sound that would announce his presence.

Both Gojang and Josira had their backs on him, hooked to the computer game as junkies to drugs. Makol sat on a chair near the door and watched their backs with the rising anger of a deranged victim. At one point, Pastor Gojang was so overwhelmed by the brilliance of a move Josira had made that he cried, 'tough girl!' hugged and kissed her straight on her lips – a rather over stretched kiss for the moment. Josira threw away the cell phone in her hand and clung to him dragging him on top of her. 'Oh Pastor,' she moaned aloud. 'How I wish this is in your church – our rolling sack.'

Whenever Gojang was making love to her, she loved calling him Pastor while in the act. It was her way of spiting defiance at God. Gojang's hand reached for his fly button then he stiffened. His eyes had just strayed into the demented eyes of Makol blazing the fury of Gorgon Medusa.[*]

Josira not yet aware of the situation had slipped out of her lower wears from her back-lying position on the floor. She was making to sit up to take off her upper wears when the rigidity in Gojang and the fixation of his eyes on a farther object communicated themselves to her. Following his eyes, she encountered the typhoon that was Makol's face. All sex went out of her like water

---

[*] One of three fabled female monsters of horrifying and petrifying aspect, winged with hissing serpents for hair.

through a sieve. A tiny scream rose to her mouth, but met a dry throat.

'Go on barge her,' Makol said, surprisingly calmer in voice than the look on his face 'I am only an uninterested spectator, I don't mean harm.'

Pastor Gojang made to stand up. Makol drew his gun and leveled it at him.

'I say go on, barge her. Was that not what you were about? I hate being a killjoy, and I am not about changing a life policy. Man, go on; deliver your goods to depot.'

But Josira the depot owner had, unknown to Makol whose eyes were fixed on the straddled form of Gojang, gone through Gojang's legs to hide behind him like behind a pillar of cloud in heaven. When Makol discovered this on looking down, he commanded Gojang to step aside. Gojang did delivering Josira's nudity to Makol who by the look on his face did not seem to see her.

'Before the count of three, I want the two of you out of your clothes and back to the floor for the unfinished business.'

He didn't have to count two times before both Gojang and Josira stood *in puris naturalibus** before him. The look on his face and the vicious looking gun in his hand could have obtained obedience from the devil.

---

* *Quite naked.*

'*Oyah*, get on with the fireworks! Deliver the weapons on target!' he commanded. Again, Pastor Gojang did not move, but Josira closed in on him and swallowed him up in a stiff embrace. Gojang waited for that stir in his shrub that might deliver him from the jam he was in, but none came though Josira was busy doing things to him. He strained himself to attain that deliverance, but failed to provoke any excitement of the type required of him. He gave up and waited for Makol's pleasure. It took a long time in coming. He seemed to be debating something in his mind. Whatever it was, it did not seem to hold happy prospects for the two orphans of lust.

'The two of you, come here,' he commanded at last.

Gojang reached for his trousers.

'Hey!'

Gojang stood still.

'If you as much as stretch out your filthy fingers for anything again, I will use your blood to flush your contamination of this house,' he swore, built-up emotions in him making him pant. 'Now, move!'

Gojang and Josira moved to the table.

'Sit down and let's talk like our kind of friends can talk.'

They both sat down. To Pastor Gojang he first turned.

'Pastor!' he called in the loud manner a mother might call her child that had wandered into the neighborhood.

Pastor Gojang shrank from the whip of the title.

'Some age, some pastors,' Makol said. 'I thought I had seen degeneration in my life, I didn't know what I have seen is the mere foam of it. Some *kaliyuga* state we are indeed. A Pastor sleeping with a woman right inside the church? Ah!' he cried overwhelmed by the weirdness of it all. 'Man, what kind of pastor are you?'

'A Pastor of the flock of Christ.'

'Of the cunts of women you mean?'

Pastor Gojang did not say anything.

'What do you preach in your church?'

'I preach salvation.'

'From sex starvation?'

No answer came from Pastor Gojang.

'What is your name?'

'Gojang.'

'Goliard you mean?'

Pastor Gojang sighed.

'What is the name of your church?'

'Give Christ the Glory Church.'

'Or Give Gojang the Girls Church?'

Gojang remained mute.

'What took you into the Christ ministry?'

'To win souls for Christ.'

'And you are winning them in the cunts of women?'

'Gojang kept quiet.'

'I want an answer to this question and I don't intend to wait for it.'

'Truly, I went into the ministry to make money like my friend Wollia.'

'So, in addition to Give Gojang the Girls Church, we have Give Gojang the Golden Calf?* Man! you are some wonder. You know what? you represent the vilest incarnation of evil I have ever come across. To dance with the devil in the very temple of God to me shows a lost soul that is out of touch with all forms of order. Even my good for nothing father, Mimono wouldn't do a thing like that. It is the aberration of ...'

'Mimono, Mimono, Mimono,' Josira intoned, then cried, 'Lonkoj!'

Makol nearly jumped out of his skin. 'Josira,' he called. She rushed towards him, but Makol raised his gun.

'No use Josira. Though we are twins, I have to kill you as I will surely kill your Pastor lover. There is nothing you have done in your life in the way of a sister that can excite love in me. You are in no closer ties to me than the cur by your side,' he said in a softer but more bitter tone. The memories he was recalling were memories he would have preferred forgotten.

'You killed our mother when she came back from the church because of a fever that would not

---

* *Wealth, as an object of worship.*

allow her stay to the end of the all-night revival prayer to find you and the wretch who called himself our father making passionate love. You didn't see her, neither did he. She walked away a forlorn woman who had been stabbed in the heart by her own daughter. That night, she slept under a tree in the severe cold of the harmattan, her fever moving to a crisis. She never recovered from that fever. I who was closer to her, was left with people who were supposed to be my closest relations, but who were total strangers to me. While I pinned in hunger and sorrow, you and our swine of a father were swooning in sex in our seedy home. I had to run away from home to roam the streets where a Good Samaritan took me to his house and educated me up to part one in the university before armed robbers broke into our house and shot him and his wife dead. I was left with four children of my benefactor, two of whom were about my age, and the other two by far my seniors. The two elderly children feeling I was a liability to them, threw me out into the streets again. Having no one to turn to, I had to drop out of the university and roam the streets of Pawadaku where I later got into the Dametan Police Force.

'Throughout my life, one memory had haunted me: the memory of the circumstances of my mother's death and your complicity in it. A majestic contempt for women arose in me and I longed for the day I will even the scores with them. It came while I was with the Police Force. A little girl was brought to our station to be taken to a reformatory for some delinquent behavior of hers. I took her to my office on the last floor of the station for a reformation of her mustard pot, which I felt was the evil wine corrupting her manners. I was caught, tried, and jailed for twenty-one years. I broke jail and went into highbrow crime. It was in it I met you.

'In my entire life, only two women had managed to climb over the fence of my ill-will for womankind into my heart. Your evil self and Ninatu whom, perhaps, I didn't stay long enough with to discover the kind of devil she was. I doted on you and would have not been happier for anything than being married to you. Little did I know the queen of my heart was a slut of a sister in unholy coition with a randy Pastor. Your infamy cast you asunder to the realm of demons and I cannot harbor love for demons. To think I was contemplating breaking ranks with my comrades to....

'OK, OK,' The Prince said, coming into the room with the swagger of an imperial monarch. 'We have waited for too long outside. Cold is eating into my skull. I think, it is time for me to chip in something in your parley.'

Following him like an imperial Japanese wedding train, were Yomoyo, Dikask and Jirimi.

Chapter Thirty

For all the surprise the Prince sought to spring, as far as Makol was concerned, it was as good as if he had not walked in. There was no change of expression of any kind on Makol's face. Gojang's face went a shade paler, but Josira was a neurotic wreck.

The Prince had for the past three days been intensively investigating Makol's social relationships and had turned up his intimate affair with Josira. Tracing her house presented no difficulty to him whose specialty was such assignment. Having located her home, he decided to act fast. Makol was now a security risk to him and the Brotherhood at this sensitive period of abducting people into the world of Cimmeri. There was no telling what Makol would blab out between Josira's laps. 'The fear of Delilah,' the Prince told himself, 'is the beginning of wisdom.' Though, he treasured Makol's skills and expertise, in the face of his flirtation with their common doom, his abilities were of no moment. Without telling the other Cimmerians what their mission that night was, he had brought them first to learn from Makol's misadventure, and secondly, to assist in dispatching him to *the bay of witches*. Apart from the fact that he knew the capabilities of Makol and doubted his ability to handle him alone without surprise working in his favor, the torturous manner he wanted to proceed against Makol required others' assistance. When he had left Cimmeri with his men, they had gone straight to Josira's apartment with the intention of abducting her, taking her to Makol's house, raping her before him and then carving the two of them to death with their barbecue knives. They arrived Josira's premises at the time Makol shouted *Pastor!*' The epithet *Pastor* like an *ignis fatuus,** nearly deflected their advance to the house. The Prince merely acting on intelligence began to doubt the accuracy of his intelligence. For the first time, a big chink was gaping in the armor of his plan. He knew why. He had not confirmed his intelligence before acting. This, he also knew why. The urgency of the present task did not make allowance for confirmation.

But then the voice sounds like that of Makol, he reasoned. 'What of it? What is the difference between a pastor today and an armed robber, except that one is using a gun to rob and the other is using the Bible?' he said and issued a laughter a rat might mistake for the cry of a cat. For a while, his mind flashed back to his experience in Gojang's church then flitted back to the task on hand. A pastor should be in the company of a man like Makol sitting on money he thought issuing the same cat-like laughter. On the strength of this reasoning, he whispered to the

---

** Light that leads travelers out of their way: Shakespeare's Henry IV part I Act 3 scene III.*

other Cimmerians to wait for him while he tiptoed to the front door. Peeping through a curtain opening of the slightly opened door, his eyes fell on Makol's back and Josira's naked breast. He knew Makol's back like he knew the paths of Cimmeri. Like a shadow, he withdrew back to the other Cimmerians and together they tiptoed back to the house to listen to the unfolding drama.

The Prince now had the advantage of standing by a wider curtain opening than the one he first peeped through. Through the new opening, he took in all that went on inside the house. Neither he nor his men suffered any impatience standing outside and listening to Makol's tale of differences with women. But when it appeared their comrade was about spilling the beans to those who had rubbed him the wrong way, the Prince decided he had had enough.

'Parleys are not for loonies,' Makol said, his eyes narrowing to a darker shade. Whenever he looked this way, he was a lethal bomb. His mind was very busy. He knew the game was up. The way the Prince spoke told him he had eavesdropped on all he had said to Josira. He, for one, did not fear the Prince. In a one-on-one duel he knew he could take on the Prince any day, anytime. But now he had to reckon with the other three Cimmerians. He knew he could no more take on the four men than he could turn invisible and disappear from the room. Curiously even with this knowledge, he experienced no quickening of the heart. Unconsciously he had resolved to fight them to his death if it came to that and he was sure it had come to that. He was particularly thankful that apart from his gun, which was fully loaded, his throwing knife was by his waist band. He savoured a secret triumph when by flicking his eyes, he discovered that with the exception of Yomoyo, the Prince and his other men had their weapons somewhere other than in their hands.

'Interesting,' the Prince said, moving nearer Makol. Then he saw Pastor Gojang and instantly recognized him, but pretended not to. He also recognized Josira as the sophisticated lady he saw in Give Christ the Glory Church, but also pretended not to, saving his knowledge of them for a distraction he might need later in this tricky encounter. Pastor Gojang and Josira in their turn recognized the Prince the moment he entered the room, but far from getting relief by his coming, they were further alarmed.

'How sad that all your life you have always lived under the shadow of beeheaded strikers,' he continued addressing Makol. 'I have always thought you stand close to me in intellect; little did I know your brain is that of a little bird pecking at camwood that has no worms.'

'If you move another step towards me, it will be the last in your twisted life,' Makol said, and to the shock and bewilderment of the Prince, a snickersnee knife jumped into Makol's right hand where the gun he held was and the gun went to his left hand. He was facing the Prince and the other Cimmerians, his back to Josira and Gojang. In different circumstances, this time was the most auspicious time for Gojang and Josira to work for their escape. But, as if by telepathic communication, both had a common understanding Makol was a kinder evil than the Prince and his Cimmerian brothers. They remained seated where they were in their nudity.

The Prince knew the implication of disobeying Makol's command. He stopped in his tracks.

Dikask who stood to the left of Makol was moving his right hand gradually towards his beltline when Makol caught the movement with the tail of his left eye and that was where the hand stopped. A smart throw of his knife by Makol drove it firmly into his guts. He coughed blood twice then tumbled down in a bloody heap.

Gojang and Josira exchanged glances of surprise and terror. The Prince was mad, but there was nothing he could do with his gun still firmly in his waistband. In a moment of madness and over confidence – something he had always warned his Cimmerian brothers to avoid, he and his men had walked in without drawing their guns. Now with his best man gone, the fear of falling victim to the vice of over-confidence haunted him. Makol had the choice of shooting Dikask with his gun, but chose to knife him to death. The implication of that choice was not lost on the Prince. By risking a miss through a knife throw, Makol was sending a message of his abiding lethal capabilities to him and his fellows. Bits of sweat shone on his face. Perhaps this was the time to employ distraction. 'Pastor,' he called pastor Gojang

Pastor Gojang full of contempt for the Prince even in his present situation did not say anything.

Makol knowing the Prince listened in from outside must have overheard him calling Gojang pastor was not surprised by the Prince addressing Gojang with that title.

'I hope you will now follow me to Cimmeri. Forget mammon. The search for it will only bring sorrow to you,' the Prince said in a persuasive voice that was pricking Gojang like needles.

Gojang remained mute nursing his contempt with both hands.

Makol's watchful eyes remained on his fellow Cimmerians.

Moments later, Yomoyo who could only be good with his hands against a marksman like Makol moved his sluggish index finger to pull the trigger of his pistol. Again, the eagle eyes of Makol caught the movement and he shifted to the right firing simultaneously. Yomoyo's shot went off target to settle in the skull of Gojang who sat directly behind Makol before he dodged Yomoyo's shot. But Makol's two shots sank into Yomoyo's chest lifting him up and ramming him on the floor. Gojang behind was on his face on the floor, dead.

The Prince sighed; Makol hissed. Their eyes dug into each other. Something the Prince had not known for a long time in his life as a cultivated gangster fluttered in his heart. It was fear. With two of his best men gone and Makol pointing a gun at him while his own was strapped to his waist, he knew his chances had all withered. Jirimi standing by his right was no more useful to him against an immensely capable and dangerous man like Makol than the gun in his trousers waistband. Like the statue of Confucius* in Beijing, he could not fail to excite pity for the helpless from a casual acquaintance with his predicament. In desperation, he reached for Josira his second distraction device.

'And you Jezebel, what were you doing in Gojang's church the Sunday I met you there?' he asked her, his eyes keenly on Makol looking for an opening. But there was none. From the disposition of Makol he could see, his erstwhile comrade would not look to the left or to the right if he were to say the latter's dead mother was behind him. He gave up the side-tricks and engaged Makol directly. This appeared to be his only way out of the jam he had walked into with his eyes wide open.

'Makol, you know, you are my best hand; the heir-apparent to the throne of Cimmeri. Don't you think this is something we can talk over and go back to the good old days?' he pleaded.

'Like hell!' Makol hissed. 'Heir to a lunatic throne; like hell! It takes only your own kind of lunacy to imagine you can move the whole humanity into a tomb of living men. To think a mind like mine ever bought such a cranky idea,' he went on rather wretchedly. 'Presently, I think your best bet in such a crazy project is the lunkhead by your side. Such a one will follow a monkey into a farmer's trap not knowing better.' Saying this, he pumped a hail of bullets into Jirimi and went on shooting until the gun stopped. A bullet had jammed. He was now on a level playing field with the Prince who had observed his chance.

For a good part of three minutes, the two men stood looking at each other, each waiting for the other to make the first move. Four minutes on, they could hear from a distance, the siren of an approaching police vehicle. Makol forgot himself and attempted clearing the jammed bullet. The Prince's hail of bullets nearly peeled off his head completely.

Josira in a burst of terror started wailing aloud. The Prince, after pumping bullets into her, went on stabbing her until all blood drained out of her body. He wheeled round looking for the ghost of Makol to vent vengeance on. The siren of the police was moving nearer and nearer. Not seeing

Makol's ghost, he ran out of the house. He yanked open pastor Gojang's car thinking it was the vehicle that brought them. Then he saw their car a little far off and ran to it. But the keys were not with him. They were with Jirimi who drove them. He ran back into the house to get the keys. In a deranged state, he could not consider the merits and demerits of attempting an escape in a car at that hour of the night when there were very few vehicles on the road and the police were apparently moving in his direction.

When he got into the house, Yomoyo was making to sit up. Believing him to be the ghost of Makol, the Prince emptied the remaining bullets in his gun into him. Rolling the dead body of Jirimi, he found the bunch of keys, picked it and ran out of the house again. As the engine of the car revved into life, the light of the police jeep picked up the car. A violent reverse to take a side street horizontal to the one the police vehicle was coming from, rammed his rear tyres into a ditch he had not seen. Accelerating forward, the sound of the engine and the squeals of the spinning tyres rivaled the police siren. Instead of moving, the car was digging in. Slateloose, the Prince flung open the door of the car and came out as the police van pulled up a couple of yards away.

What of it? the Prince thought. I have money. It is the bones I will throw to the dogs of the cabal. There was a visible improvement in his composure as he walked towards the police.

The Police, like the vultures of Parsee*
country, waited patiently for him. Like all
Dametans, they had a price. They would pick his
flesh if he could not pay their price. But if he
could, why should they embarrass him? They
might even be his nest.

* The Parsees in India practiced tree-burial for their dead. The body of a
dead Parsee was left on a tree for vultures and other birds of prey to
pick the flesh leaving the bones. Their slogan for this type of burial
was: flesh to the skies, bones to the earth.